"You'
such a
kisses. "...u u use anyone to get what
you want, wouldn't you?"

No, she couldn't have heard him correctly.
What was he talking about?

"Now, I'm going to use you."

"No! No, Jed. Stop! I don't want this!
Please!"

"Why should I listen to you," he rasped.
"You've spent your whole life taking advantage of others. It's about time someone took advantage of you."

Caitlin felt frozen. This couldn't be happening! This wasn't the Jed she knew.

Then suddenly he stopped. "No, I can't! I can't do it, even to you!" In one quick action, he flung himself away from her.

Why, oh, why, she sobbed uncontrollably. Why had he done this to her?

Bantam Books in the Caitlin Series

LOVING
LOVE LOST

LOVE LOST

Created by
Francine Pascal

Written by
Joanna Campbell

BANTAM BOOKS
TORONTO · NEW YORK · LONDON · SYDNEY · AUCKLAND

RL 5, IL age 12 and up

LOVE LOST

A Bantam Book / September 1985

Conceived by Francine Pascal

*Produced by Cloverdale Press Inc.,
133 Fifth Avenue, New York, N.Y. 10003*

*Starfire and accompanying logo of a stylized star
are trademarks of Bantam Books, Inc.*

ISBN 0-553-25130-9

Published simultaneously in the United States and Canada

Bantam Books are published by Bantam Books, Inc. Its trademark,
consisting of the words "Bantam Books" and the portrayal of a rooster, is
Registered in U.S. Patent and Trademark Office and in other countries.
Marca Registrada. Bantam Books, Inc., 666 Fifth Avenue, New York,
New York 10103.

PRINTED IN THE UNITED STATES OF AMERICA

O   0 9 8 7 6 5 4 3 2 1

1

"I can't go riding today, Ginny," Caitlin Ryan said as she finished tying her shining black hair back with a scarlet silk scarf. She turned to her roommate, Ginny Brookes. "I'm going over to the Fosters'."

"Again? You were over there yesterday."

"Ian needs lots of encouragement."

Ginny pulled her jodhpurs up over her long legs and fastened them, then pinned her straight light brown hair haphazardly to the top of her head and set her velvet hard hat in place over it. "With all the time you're spending with him lately, I'd think Jed'd be pretty jealous."

At the mention of her boyfriend's name, Caitlin's blue eyes sparkled. "I'll see him tonight. We're going to study for finals together. He thinks it's great that I'm helping Ian."

"Are you making any more progress?"

Caitlin sighed sadly. "Not really. It's so hard for a six year-old to understand that if he's' going to get better, he has to work hard at it."

"Dean and Mrs. Foster are lucky to have you

1

around, but you're sure missing some good riding!" Ginny picked up her crop from the dresser. "I'd better go. Bert's meeting me at the stables."

But as she reached for the doorknob, she paused and looked back at her friend. "You know, Jed's really been good for you."

"Oh?"

"Well, you've changed—for the better, that is. Eight months ago the last thing I'd expected you to do was take care of a sick little boy."

"Oh, Ginny," Caitlin said scornfully. For an instant she frowned. She couldn't stop herself from thinking back to the accident that had crippled Ian Foster and shocked the entire Highgate Academy campus—the maintenance shed that had been left unlocked . . . the poisonous chemicals the little boy had ingested and the fall he'd taken as a result. Diana Chasen, the student baby-sitter who'd been blamed, had left school because of it. Then Caitlin shook herself and laughed. "You just never bothered to look at my finer qualities."

"Right! I'll see you later."

As Ginny rushed out, banging the door behind her, Caitlin crossed the blue-carpeted room and went to the desk to pick up the new book she'd bought for Ian. Then she, too, hurried out of the girls' dormitory building and into the warm, early June sunshine.

Her strides were long and graceful as she crossed the green lawns of the Highgate campus toward the dignified brick classroom buildings. The private school had once been a prosperous

Virginia plantation, and its elegance and old-world grace still clung to its vine-covered walls.

Breathing in the sweet-scented spring air, Caitlin smiled to herself. She couldn't remember having ever been so happy. The last few months had been the absolute best in her life. Ginny was right; Jed Michaels had turned her world around.

Everything seemed so much brighter to Caitlin since they'd started going together several months before. Jed was so good and so caring, giving her the love she'd longed for for so long. None of the many boys she'd dated had ever made her feel so special or so wanted.

Immersed in her dreamy thoughts, Caitlin didn't hear someone coming up behind her. Suddenly she was grabbed by the waist and lifted nearly a foot off the ground.

"Hi, there, beautiful," a deep, slightly drawling voice said in her ear. "Did I surprise you?"

"Oh, Jed! You scared me," she cried. But as he set her back on the ground, she was glowing. She turned around to face him. "I'm on my way to the Fosters'," she added.

"I know. My science meeting got over early, so I thought I'd walk you over. That okay?"

"Sure. I'd give you a kiss, but somebody might see."

"Later," he whispered, his green eyes dancing with promise.

Even though Caitlin had memorized every inch of his ruggedly handsome face, from his wavy, light brown hair to the cleft in his strong chin, she still felt tingly all over every time she looked at him.

He smiled crookedly. "What's that you've got? A new book for Ian?"

She nodded. "He liked the last one so much. I couldn't resist."

Jed had grown more serious as he gazed down at her. "I'm glad you're going over there and helping him. You don't have to do it."

She laughed and linked her arm through his. "I don't mind. He's a real cutie."

Jed's expression darkened. "That's what Diana used to say. No one's heard a word from her since she left. I hope you're not doing this because of what she and I went through. You don't have to feel responsible—"

"Of course not!" Caitlin objected a little too strongly. She hoped Jed didn't notice. "I'm doing it because I *want* to," she explained.

They started walking. The Foster home stood to the far side of the main complex. It was one of the four colonial-style faculty houses that had been designed to blend into the architecture of the old plantation.

"I'm really going to miss you this weekend," Jed said a few minutes later.

"Why? Are you going away? Jed, why didn't you tell me—"

"Whoa, there," Jed said. "I thought your grandmother was having another party with the mine people this weekend and wanted you to go."

Caitlin stopped still. "God, I can't believe I forgot about that! I was hoping you and I could finally get out and do some riding." She frowned as she continued across the lawn with Jed. "Instead, I'll have to smile my way through another boring dinner party, impressing those union people. Sometimes I wish Ryan Mining never existed."

"You probably wouldn't be here at Highgate if it didn't."

"And you and I never would have met. . . ." She looked up at him lovingly, and he pulled her arm close to his side.

"You know, I was thinking about this summer," he said quietly. "Have you asked your grandmother if you can go?"

Caitlin had been brought up by her grandmother. Her mother had died giving birth to her, and her father had abandoned her. Jed was the only person who knew the truth about her father. Caitlin told people that her father had died in an accident shortly before her birth.

"Not yet," she said. "I haven't had a chance. But I'm sure she'll say yes. She's always going on about how important it is to go out and see the world."

"But does she consider my father's ranch to be part of her world? Montana's a long way from Virginia."

"Of course she does," Caitlin said. "Anyway, whatever your place may lack in worldly sophistication, you make up for by having horses."

"Cow ponies, not thoroughbreds, Caitlin," Jed noted.

"You know that doesn't make a difference to my grandmother," Caitlin stated. "Look, why don't you come home with me this weekend? You haven't been there in a month."

He shook his head. "Not a good idea."

"Why?" Caitlin sounded hurt.

"Because I don't think that would fit in with what your grandmother's got planned."

"Come on, Jed, you know she likes you," Caitlin pleaded.

"I know. But you've got a job to do this weekend. I'd just be in the way."

Caitlin was silent for a moment. She knew he was right. "But I'll miss you."

"I'll miss you, too." They were approaching the Foster house. Jed slowed to a stop on the path outside the gate. "We'll make up for it tonight. What time should I come over?"

"Seven. Meet me in the lounge."

"See you then." He leaned over and dropped a kiss on the top of her head. "Tell Ian I said hi. I love you."

"I love you, too."

She watched as he strode back in the direction of the dorms, then she skipped up the front steps and knocked lightly on the Fosters' door.

"Is that you, Caitlin?" Mrs. Lake, the day nurse, called. "Come on in. Ian's waiting for you."

Caitlin entered and went directly to the living room.

"Come and see!" a child's voice cried out to her. "I've been drawing animals with Mrs. Lake. Here's your horse."

As Caitlin hurried forward, Mrs. Lake rose from the chair she'd positioned beside Ian's wheelchair.

6

She smiled warmly. "We've had a busy day, haven't we, Ian? We've got lots of things to tell Caitlin."

"Why, this looks just like Duster!" Caitlin exclaimed as she accepted the crayon drawing from the child.

Ian beamed with delight. "I remembered those pictures you showed me."

"You liked that book?"

"Yes." Ian nodded.

"I've got another surprise for you. Which hand do you want?" Caitlin teased as she put both behind her back, one clasping the book she'd brought.

"That one!"

"Boy, you're smart. You guessed it right off." With a flourish, Caitlin brought the gaily covered book out from behind her back and set it on the drawing board that was balanced across the arms of Ian's wheelchair. "Do you like it?"

Eagerly the boy flipped open the book to the bright pictures of African wildlife.

"What do you say, Ian?" Mrs. Lake reminded him gently.

"Thank you, Caitlin."

"You're welcome, Ian. We can read it now."

"Well, I'd better be going," Mrs. Lake said. "I have to pick up one of my daughters from a softball game. Ian tried out that new exercise today—the one I showed you. If you could work with him a few minutes this afternoon—"

"No!" Ian looked up from his book and scowled. "I don't like them. They hurt!"

7

"I know, Ian," Caitlin sympathized, "but if we're going to make your legs strong again, it's going to hurt a little. We'll make a game of it like we did the other day."

Ian's expression grew a little less mutinous. Mrs. Lake nodded and smiled in approval. "I'll see you tomorrow morning, Ian."

"'Bye, Mrs. Lake."

"'Bye, Ian. 'Bye, Caitlin. Keep up the good work."

As Mrs. Lake let herself out the front door, Caitlin sat down in the chair beside Ian. "Let's go back to the first page, and I'll read to you for a while. . . ."

Thirty minutes later, having read half the book to him, with the promise of finishing it the next day, Caitlin put the book aside and removed the drawing board from Ian's wheelchair.

"Time to try your exercises."

"No! I don't want to!"

"Don't you want to show me how strong you are?"

Ian continued to frown at her stubbornly.

"Afterward we'll have something to eat—cookies and ice cream, maybe?"

"With chocolate syrup?"

"Maybe even a double scoop."

Ian was definitely looking more cooperative.

"Now this is the game I thought up," Caitlin hurried on quickly before she lost his interest. "We'll pretend we're in Africa, looking for all those animals we saw in the book. Every time you do your exercise, you get to choose two animals that will be yours. After we get done, we'll draw them and hang them up to show how good you are. Okay?"

"Can I pick elephants?"

"Whatever you want. Now I'm going to lay you down on the floor, Ian. Then we're going to lift up each of your legs and try to bend them as far as they'll go." Caitlin picked Ian up and gently settled him on the carpeted floor.

"Ready?" She gripped his foot and ankle and slowly pushed so that his leg bent at the knee.

"Ow," Ian cried, immediately fighting against her.

"Just think—not only an elephant, but something else, too. What do you want? A lion?"

"A rhinocerous."

"Good! Just a little more. Wonderful! Ian's got two animals. Now that wasn't so bad, was it?"

Ian grinned.

"Let's try the other leg. What animals do you want this time?"

"A tiger."

"Tigers don't live in Africa, but that's okay. We'll make believe they do. And how about a hippopotamus?"

"Okay."

For fifteen minutes Caitlin worked with Ian, and with each tiny bit of progress he made, she felt something inside herself healing, too.

As she lifted Ian back into his wheelchair, she gave him a huge smile. "You've done such a good job today, I think you deserve an extra scoop of ice cream. What do you think?"

"Yes! And chocolate syrup!"

"I don't think your mother will mind. Let's go into the kitchen, and while we're eating, we can start drawing your animals. Sound good?"

Ian nodded his small blond head eagerly. "I wish you were here all the time, Caitlin."

Caitlin took Ian's hand and squeezed it. "I wish I were too, Ian. But I'll always be your friend."

It felt so good to Caitlin's aching conscience to be able to help and care for this little boy. But it would take such a long time for him to get better—*if* he got better at all. Would she ever be free from the guilt that nagged at her? And how would Ian feel if he knew the truth—that Caitlin had been the one responsible for the accident that had crippled him? She shook her head quickly to force the thoughts away. No, she wouldn't think about it! She couldn't!

2

Because of the beautiful weather, a group of juniors had taken their lunches out to the front lawn of the campus the following day. "I've got the most totally gorgeous dress for the junior prom!" one of them, Morgan Conway, bubbled.

"Really?" Gloria Parks asked. "What's it look like?"

"I'm not telling. You'll probably go out and get one just like it."

"You know I wouldn't do that, Morgan," Gloria said, pretending to sound hurt. Turning to Caitlin, she called, "How are the plans for the prom coming?"

Caitlin and Jed were leaning their backs against the trunk of one of the ancient oak trees, sharing their lunches. "You'd better ask Roger. I put him in charge of the prom committee several weeks ago. They don't even need me to check on how they're doing anymore. Right, Roger?" She teasingly winked at the handsome junior and star athlete sitting a few yards away. "If he's going to run for

11

student council president next year, he needs the practice."

"Aren't *you* running again, Caitlin?" Morgan paused with her sandwich halfway to her mouth.

"One year as president is enough. Someone else should have the chance. Besides"—she cast a look toward Jed—"I'll have a lot to keep me busy next year."

"I'll bet!" Gloria shot out.

But Jed laughingly interrupted her. "So tell us how it's going, Roger."

"Well, Caitlin got the band and caterer before I took over. The decorations and seating arrangements are all set, and I just sent the ballots for the king and queen to the printer. I was going to drop that bit, but they wouldn't let me."

"We always have a king and queen," Morgan reminded him. "It's tradition."

"A dumb one, if you ask me. Don't you guys think so?" Roger looked to the other boys for support.

Tim Collins shrugged. "I won't be wearing the crown, so I don't care."

"You guys just don't understand," Gloria said. "This is not just a dance—it's the biggest social event of the year."

"Besides," Morgan said with a touch of cattiness, "we already can guess who are going to be picked king and queen." She stared pointedly at Jed and Caitlin.

"I'm going to vote for you and Roger," Caitlin said without blinking an eye.

Morgan flushed as some of the others started to laugh.

"We'll all find out the night of the prom," Ginny said diplomatically.

"And don't forget my party afterward," Brett Perkins said. He and Dorothy Raite were sitting a little to the side of the others and had been engrossed in their own conversation. Brett, with his tall, dark looks, and Dorothy, sleek and blond, had been inseparable since Caitlin had gotten them together a few months before.

"How are you getting everyone out to the island?" Jed asked. "That's a lot of shuffling."

"My parents' cabin cruiser. We can carry eight at a time."

"You didn't invite the whole class, did you?" Gloria said in amazement.

"Are you serious? My parents would kill me. I invited about thirty, but there'll probably end up being a few more than that."

"Just think," Gloria exclaimed, "only two more weeks, and I'll be in Europe!"

"Again?" Caitlin casually shined her apple on the leg of Jed's jeans.

"My parents want to do a canal trip through the Loire Valley this year. Then we'll go on to our place on the coast. What about you? Your grandmother must have another one of her fantastic trips planned."

"No. I'm going out to Montana with Jed."

"You are?"

"My father invited her to join us this summer,"

13

Jed explained. "We're going to turn her into a cowgirl."

"Caitlin?" Morgan gasped. "She'll be the first cowgirl in jodhpurs. Are you sure you can handle the Wild West, Caitlin?"

"We're just as civilized as you are," Jed said.

Caitlin frowned. "I think it will be great."

"But definitely *not you*," Morgan teased. "You might break one of those perfectly manicured nails."

Caitlin deliberately ignored the last remark as she and Jed, both thinking of the plans they'd made together, shared a secret look.

"And what great things are you doing this summer, Morgan?" Ginny called out.

"Oh, we'll be going to our place in Maine and get in some sailing," Morgan said matter-of-factly. "Daddy's bought a forty-five-foot Hinkley. We'll be doing a lot of racing."

Jed had checked his watch and started to get up. "Caitlin, we'd better get going if we want to stop in the library before class. See you all later."

" 'Bye, everyone." She smiled at him and rose, slinging her knapsack over her shoulder. As they started away from the others, she said in an undertone, "That Morgan can be such a cat."

"Don't pay any attention to her. She's just jealous."

"Of me?"

"You're pretty, you're popular, and you're a good person besides."

"And I've got you."

"You sure have." He winked down at her, and

14

with shoulders touching, they walked toward the library.

Caitlin wasn't at all happy about having to go home for the weekend, but as Rollins, her grandmother's driver and the butler at Ryan Acres, headed the Bentley down the long avenue of trees leading to the house, she forced herself to look cheerful. She knew her grandmother would make some kind of scolding comment if she dared to walk in with a long face.

Rollins pulled to a stop before the imposing, white-columned front of the house. Quickly he came around to open the rear door for Caitlin.

"Thanks, Rollins." Her smile was warm and genuine. "I'll go on in and say hello to my grandmother. Margaret can bring my bag up."

"Very well, Miss Ryan."

Caitlin hurried up the steps and through the open double front doors into the marble-floored foyer of the house. She paid little attention to the fine furnishings and museum-quality paintings on the walls as she stepped across the thick Persian carpet, past the curving staircase. Her destination was her grandmother's study at the end of the hall.

Caitlin knocked on the door and waited for her grandmother's answer. She was just about to knock again when a maid came into the hall from the servants' wing.

"Oh, Miss Ryan. It's good to see you," Margaret said. "If you're looking for Mrs. Ryan, she went out to the stables."

"Thanks, Margaret. Guess I'll go out and meet her there. Have her guests arrived?"

"The Lowerys and some friends of theirs have arrived. She's showing them the horses."

Caitlin nodded. "I just have a small bag. Rollins left it in the hall."

"I'll bring it up."

As Margaret walked away, Caitlin glanced down at her clothing and wondered if she should change. Her grandmother was so particular about what she wore. After a moment's thought she decided not to. The cotton skirt and blousy tunic she'd put on before she left the dorm were both stylish and girlish enough to please her grandmother. She smoothed her hair, walked down the long hallway, then went out through the French doors of the breakfast room and across the lush back lawns toward the stables. A crew was working on the swimming pool, readying it for the summer. They looked up curiously as she passed, but she ignored them.

Jeff, the stable hand, greeted her as she entered the huge barn. At another time Caitlin would have paused to chat with him about the horses, but she didn't want to keep her grandmother waiting. "They're down at the end, looking over the new mare." He smiled.

"Thanks, Jeff."

As she headed down between the rows of stalls, her eyes adjusted to the dimmer light in the barn. She saw her grandmother, tall and slim in a tailored blue riding habit, every silver hair on her head neatly in place. With her were four others:

Bob Lowery, president of the mineworkers' union, and his wife, Barbara, whom Caitlin recognized, and another couple about the same age.

Regina Ryan threw back her head and laughed at something Mr. Lowery said. "Yes, at the cost of grain, we should feed them from the table, but I do love it. Riding is such a pleasant escape from my worries at the office. Ah, here's my granddaughter." She scowled slightly. "You didn't stop to change, Caitlin? We *are* riding."

Caitlin suddenly realized they were all in riding attire. She improvised quickly. "I thought I'd come out and say hello first before changing."

"She's so thoughtful." Mrs. Ryan smiled at the others. "Well, come give me a kiss. You know the Lowerys, of course. And this is Ed Jankowitz and his wife, Mary. Ed is visiting from union headquarters in Washington. My granddaughter, Caitlin."

Caitlin extended her hand. "How do you do, Mr. and Mrs. Jankowitz? Nice to see you again, Mr. and Mrs. Lowery."

"Good to see you, too, Caitlin. How's school coming?" Bob Lowery asked. "Getting pretty close to summer vacation, I'll bet."

Caitlin grinned. "School is great. I've really enjoyed it this year."

"That was some production you put on last fall."

"Oh, the fund-raiser. Yes, we had fun."

"I got a kick out of it. You did a good job."

"Thank you, Mr. Lowery."

"Yes, I must say I am proud of her talent." Mrs. Ryan tapped Caitlin's shoulder lightly and beamed at her guests. "I was so sorry to have missed her school production, but business interfered, as it too often does. Since you haven't changed"— Regina was still smiling, but she gave Caitlin a mild reprimanding look—"we'll go on ahead. I do hate to keep our guests waiting."

"It won't take me but a minute," Caitlin said apologetically.

"There's no need to bother now," Mrs. Ryan said. "We're only going for a short ride. You might as well wait and join us for dinner. The Turners won't be joining us until then."

Mrs. Ryan turned quickly back to her guests. "Ed, Bob, I have the horses already waiting out in the paddock. Mary, I know you wanted a quiet mount . . ."

Regina Ryan was already shepherding her guests off. The Lowerys and the Jankowitzes waved to Caitlin in parting, but Caitlin felt as if she'd done something wrong again—and she didn't know what it was.

Caitlin dressed with care for dinner in a softly tailored, royal blue, silk dress, belted at the waist. She wore a single strand of pearls around her neck. She won her grandmother's subtle but approving nod as she joined her and their guests in the elegant living room before dinner.

Although the June night was warm, decorative fires were burning in the marble fireplaces at each end of the high-ceilinged room, adding a touch of coziness to the ice green and peach decor and gilded Louis XIV furnishings.

"I was just saying to Mr. and Mrs. Lowery," her grandmother advised Caitlin as she accepted the glass of Perrier Rollins offered, "that they should bring their son and daughter to Ryan Acres this summer for a visit. They would be wonderful company for you, dear. Riding, swimming, and tennis here, and, of course, you would all go to the country club. We often go off for a few weeks—the heat can be *so* oppressive here in Virginia in the summer—but unfortunately I'll be much too busy with mining business to take Caitlin away this year. How old did you say your children were, Barbara? Thirteen and sixteen?"

Caitlin tried to pay attention to the rest of their conversation. She nodded and smiled in the right places, but her heart had stopped at her grandmother's comment. What was her grandmother going to say when Caitlin told her about the plans she and Jed had made?

She had to put those thoughts out of her mind as they sat down to dinner in the formal dining room at the opposite side of the front foyer. Malcolm Turner, the head of Underwood Mining, walked her in. His wife was ill that evening, and he'd come alone. He was a sweet, kind man with five children of his own, two of them daughters her age, and he always took an interest in Caitlin. Still Caitlin felt out of place at the table full of adults where the conversation centered on business.

Yet despite Caitlin's worries, the rest of the weekend went so smoothly that her grandmother was in a cheerful, expansive mood when her guests had departed and she and Caitlin sat down to a late brunch Sunday.

"Well, the weekend was definitely a success." Mrs. Ryan smiled as she poured herself a cup of coffee from the silver pot Margaret had left on the table. "I'm sure Mr. Lowery is beginning to see things my way, and we'll get some of those concessions from the union."

"I'm glad to hear that," Caitlin agreed automatically. Caitlin was glowing, too, but not from anything that had happened at Ryan Acres. Jed had called her from campus the night before just to say hello and to tell her that he missed her. Fortunately the call had come while they'd been dressing for dinner, so Caitlin had been able to talk freely and at length. She'd told him of her worries and of her grandmother's plans for her that summer; and in his wonderful, comforting way, he'd told her to sit tight, confident that things would work out for them. He'd see her when she got back to the dorm at six that evening.

"We haven't had a chance to chat at all this weekend." Mrs. Ryan's voice broke into Caitlin's thoughts. "You look happy this morning. You enjoyed yourself?"

"Very much."

"What have you been doing at school? I received an excellent report from the dean on your grades."

"I've been working hard. We just finished our tennis season. Our team finished second behind Arsworth—but you know they always win. And I've been helping the Fosters' little boy, Ian. You remember I told you how he'd been paralyzed from the waist down after the accident?"

"Yes. How could I forget the scandal—it was all the fault of that scholarship girl you had as a guest here once. She never should have been at Highgate. Why, she had no background at all. I must make a point of bringing up the school's screening procedures at the next board meeting." Mrs. Ryan snorted as she took a sip from her cup. "In any case, the dean did mention something about your visiting his son. It's a thoughtful gesture on your part, but surely you're not spending all your free time over there?"

"No, not all of it. Ginny and I have been riding some, and I have a great idea for this summer. Jed's father asked me out to their ranch. I told him I had to ask you, but that I thought you'd say yes.

Regina Ryan paused with her cup in midair and stared at her granddaughter.

Caitlin had glanced down at her plate to gather her thoughts and didn't notice. "They have a huge house. I'd have my own bedroom. And Jed has a younger sister who's dying to meet me. It'd be a wonderful opportunity for me to see the West. Jed says we can make some side trips to Grand Teton and the Snake River . . ." Caitlin's voice drifted off.

Regina replaced her cup in the saucer.

"Can I go?" Expectation was on Caitlin's face, but inside she was nervous.

Her grandmother was silent for a long moment. The gold bracelets on her slim wrists jingled richly together as she reached for her fork. "Do you think you and Jed are becoming a bit too serious?"

"Serious?" Caitlin felt her stomach jump. "I care about him very much."

"Yes, a coltish kind of love. I remember having a few of those infatuations before I met your grandfather. Jed is a sweet boy, but you *do* have another year at Highgate and college ahead of you."

"I know that, Grandmother. We've talked about our college plans."

"Have you?" Regina studied her granddaughter for another moment, then cut into the eggs Benedict on her plate. She seemed to come to a conclusion. "We'll talk about this again after school is out."

Caitlin felt deflated. Still she pressed on. "It would be great if I could know now. Jed's father would like an answer."

"I shall have to think about it."

Caitlin took a deep breath. "Grandmother, don't you care about any of the things that are important to me? I want to go. It will really mean a lot."

"Of course I care." Mrs. Ryan cast a look across the table at Caitlin's untouched plate. "Eat something. You're still growing. Did I tell you that the Van Hornes have planned the most marvelous Fourth of July celebration. . . ."

Caitlin lifted her knife and fork, feeling defeated. Not only was her grandmother threatening to ruin her summer, but her disregard for Caitlin's feelings made her feel as significant as the bread crusts on her plate. She heaved a deep sigh. It had always been this way, and Caitlin knew there was no reason she should have believed her grandmother would start caring about what she wanted now. Still, she felt very disappointed.

3

When Caitlin arrived back at Highgate, Jed was waiting just beyond the dorm steps, leaning against one of the old oak trees.

Caitlin ran to him and flung her arms around his neck. "It was awful, awful, awful," she cried.

"What went wrong?"

"Everything," she said, still holding him close. "When I tried to talk to my grandmother about our plans, she shut me off." Caitlin shook her head as she pulled back and looked deeply into Jed's questioning eyes. "No, actually she said that you and I were too serious. She told me she'd talk to me about the trip after school gets out, but she invited the Lowery kids to spend some time this summer at Ryan Acres and to go to the club, and—oh, Jed!"

"I get the message. Do you want to take a walk before you go in? Leave your suitcase here. No one's going to take it."

Jed put his arm around her shoulder, and they started walking away from the campus buildings, past the soccer and baseball fields, toward the riding trails that covered dozens of acres behind the stable.

The glow from the sinking sun was brilliant over the western hills, casting long shadows over the fields and grass. Jed and Caitlin climbed over an old stone fence behind the stables and started walking across one of the meadows where a number of riding jumps had been set up. Jed and Caitlin had soared over them during the many afternoons they'd spent riding together.

"She didn't say no, though, did she?" Jed's arm was still about her shoulders, and he gave her a quick squeeze.

Caitlin shook her head. "But she's not going to say yes. I know her."

"Don't worry. It'll be okay." Jed looked down at her and smiled. "Even if we don't have this summer together, we'll have lots of other time. I'm not going to stop loving you."

"Oh, Jed, I know." She buried her head in his shoulder, so glad for his warmth and for his strength. "I love you, too."

"There's next year, and then college. By then she won't be making the rules for you."

"Do you think I'll ever be free? She's going to keep interfering—"

"But I'll be there to stand up for you." He kissed the top of her forehead.

They'd reached a clearing beside the path on which they were walking. There, a brook skipped down over the rocky ledges of the nearby hill in a small waterfall, then landed in a small pool. Ferns crowded about the pool's edges, and silver-backed fish could be seen continuing their trip down-stream.

"Let's sit down here," Jed suggested. "It reminds me of this place back in Montana. We used to climb up into the mountains, looking for cattle before the winter snows. There was this spot we used to camp in—a grassy meadow like this, only much bigger."

He leaned closer to her as they sat on the grass carpet, a large rock behind their backs.

The weak rays of the setting sun drifting through the trees glinted on Caitlin's hair as she leaned toward Jed.

He untied her scarf, pulled the silk fabric away, and let her thick, black hair flow over her back. "I like it much better when you wear it over your shoulders. It's so soft and pretty."

"Is that all you like?" she wondered.

"I care what's going on inside you, too. I thought you understood that."

"I do."

He regarded her. "And I don't like to see you upset. Let's just wait and see. I'll bet anything your grandmother will come around."

"Oh, Jed, what would I do without you?"

Pulling her close to him, he gave her a long, tender kiss. As always happened when they were so close, Caitlin felt a dizzy warmth flooding over her. Jed tightened his arms around her back and gently rubbed one palm up and down her spine, then tangled his fingers in her long hair.

As he drew his lips from hers to kiss her cheek, then her forehead, Caitlin sighed and snuggled closer to him. She trailed her fingers down his face to his cleft chin, then over his strong, muscled shoulder. How good it was to be close to him. How safe she felt.

Again Jed pressed his lips over hers, and they clung together in a long kiss. Then Jed moaned and gently pushed her away. Looking down at Caitlin's upturned face, he said hoarsely. "We'd better go back, before I decide to keep you here all night."

"I know," she whispered. "It would be so easy to just stay here holding each other."

"It would, but it's just going to have to wait till later. It's getting dark." He released her and rose quickly. She reached up and took his outstretched hand as she got up, then continued holding it as they started out of the clearing.

Coaching Ian every afternoon that next week took up more of Caitlin's time than she truly could spare, but working with him was one thing in her busy schedule she wasn't about to cut out.

Each time she saw his happy smile and the slow progress he was making, her heart felt warmed— and it healed just a little more.

She hurried back to the dorm after leaving the Fosters' that Thursday afternoon and bounded up the stairs. This was the first night in over a week that she wouldn't be seeing Jed and studying with him for their finals. He'd be partying at his dorm with a bunch of the guys who'd played with him on the lacrosse team. Highgate had had a successful season, and the team had good reason to celebrate.

Actually she was glad for the night alone. It would be a good time to start packing up some of the stuff in her room that would be brought back to Ryan Acres for the summer.

Thinking of the summer reminded her that her grandmother, whom she'd spoken to on the phone the evening before, had yet to tell her if she could go to Montana. In fact, Mrs. Ryan seemed to have forgotten it. And Caitlin had been too afraid of what her grandmother would say to bring it up again on her own during their phone conversation—especially since her grandmother had told her, when she'd been home for the weekend, that they'd discuss it when school was out. As she entered the room she shared with Ginny, she threw her knapsack on the lacy bedspread and went to her refrigerator for a Coke.

She opened the can, then sat down at her desk and looked around. All the furnishings were the best money could buy, arranged by a designer's hand at the insistence of her grandmother. But it was a comfortable room, and the only change Caitlin and Ginny had made was to remove the oil paintings from the walls and replace them with bright posters.

Caitlin was so immersed in her thoughts that she jumped when a quick knock sounded at the door.

"Caitlin, are you in there?"

"Emily, come on in. I'm glad you stopped by." Caitlin smiled as the pretty, curly-haired brunette stepped through the doorway. "Want a Coke? There's one in the fridge."

"Sure. Thanks."

Emily and Jed were first cousins, and Caitlin and Emily had become good friends over the course of the year. "What's up?" Caitlin asked.

"Nothing special. I was just taking a break from studying and thought I'd stop by." Emily pulled one of the overstuffed pillows off the bed and plopped down on it. But as she fiddled with her can of soda, a tiny frown formed on her brow. "Well, actually that's not true. There *is* something I wanted to tell you—but it's not good news."

"Oh?"

"I was talking to Laurence Baxter a little while ago."

Caitlin waited curiously for Emily to go on. She knew Laurence, of course. He was another junior, kind of on the quiet side but cute. He had a brilliant mind—not unlike Emily's. "So what'd he have to say?"

"He's heard from Diana. Not from her directly, but from someone who knows about her. You know how he sort of played big brother to Diana when she was here at Highgate—before the accident."

Caitlin nodded. At the mention of Diana's name, her stomach tightened. "How's she doing? She enrolled in another school, didn't she?"

"For a while. But she dropped out." Emily looked up at Caitlin with the beginnings of tears in her eyes. "She's in the hospital, Caitlin. She—she has anorexia nervosa."

"Oh, my God."

"I know. I couldn't believe it either."

"Will she be all right?"

"I hope so. I know girls who've had it and gotten better, but Laurence couldn't tell me much more. He got the news secondhand, and Diana's parents have cut off all ties with him, too—just like they have with everyone else at Highgate."

"Where is she?"

"Some hospital here in Virginia, but I'm not sure which one."

"Have you told Jed yet?"

"I haven't seen him this afternoon." Emily shook her head. "He's going to be upset. He and Diana were so close." Then she added quickly, "Oh, not like you and he are, but—"

"Don't worry, Emily, I know. He loved her like a sister." Caitlin spoke without bitterness. Jed and Diana were in the past, but the news of Diana's condition still left her trembling. She didn't dare show Emily how much—or why she was feeling so terribly responsible.

"I've asked Laurence," Emily continued, "to try to get her address. He said he would. Of course, we've only got a week before school's out. Maybe if she knew how well Ian's doing, it would help."

"I was thinking of that," Caitlin said quietly. "Will you let me know where she is if you find out?"

"Sure," Emily said. "It's so nice of you to care about her."

Oh, Emily, Caitlin thought, *if only you knew how much I care—and why.*

"Enough of this sad stuff," Emily went on, changing the subject. "Have you got your dress for the prom yet?"

Absently Caitlin nodded. "It's something I got in Paris when I was there with my grandmother last summer. It's really different—an old-fashioned ball gown."

"Sounds fabulous! Mine isn't that original. I picked it up in Georgetown one weekend, but I think Terry will like it. It's all white . . ."

As the two girls continued talking, Caitlin had trouble keeping her mind on their words. Her thoughts kept going back to Diana. How could she be in the hospital with anorexia? Leaving Highgate was supposed to have helped her put the accident behind her. What had happened?

But even as Caitlin thought this, a little voice in the back of her head was chiding her with the terrible realization that she knew exactly what had happened. Diana was still suffering with guilt over the accident she thought she had caused—and only Caitlin knew Diana was blameless.

4

Five minutes before the end of Caitlin's last class the next day, one of the assistants from the dean's office stepped into the American history classroom and left a note on the teacher's desk.

Mr. Walters was at the blackboard writing out a study list for the final exam and only nodded to the assistant. "I have a message here for you, Caitlin, from your grandmother," he called out a moment later. "Stop by my desk before you leave."

"Okay, Mr. Walters." She gave the teacher a warm smile, but inside she was concerned. It was Friday afternoon, and it was not uncommon for her grandmother to summon her to spend the weekend at Ryan Acres on such short notice. It was the last thing Caitlin felt like doing.

She finished copying the study list, closed her notebook, and as the bell rang hurried up to Mr. Walter's desk. He handed her the pink message slip, and she paused by his desk to read it. "Your grandmother would like you to come directly to the front steps of the main builiding."

Caitlin frowned. What did her grandmother

want? She nodded her thanks to Mr. Walters and left the room, nearly walking into Morgan and Gloria, who were standing right outside the door talking.

"Boy, you're in a hurry," Morgan said. "Where are you going?"

"To the main building. My grandmother's here to see me."

"Oh, really?" Gloria was immediately intrigued. Everyone at Highgate knew about Caitlin's rich and powerful grandmother and were a little awed by her. "What for?"

Caitlin shrugged. "I don't know." Then for the other girls' benefit she flashed a dazzling smile. "But knowing Grandmother, it'll be wonderful."

Caitlin would never let anyone at the school know that her relationship with Regina Ryan was not as loving and warm as she painted it to be. The only person who knew the whole truth was Jed, whom Caitlin would have trusted with her life.

"We'll come with you," Morgan said.

Caitlin seemed to consider it for a second. "You'd better not. My grandmother might not like being surrounded by a whole bunch of kids."

"We're not exactly a 'bunch,'" Morgan argued.

"Caitlin's right," Gloria observed. "This is between her and her grandmother."

"I'd better get going." Caitlin lifted a hand in parting, then started off down the hall. "See you later."

She quickened her pace and hurried out the door into the warm June sunshine. The lawns were crowded as she followed one of the brick pathways toward the main building, which had been the original plantation house. Roger Wake tried to get her attention on the way. "I need to talk to you about prom flowers," he called.

"Not now, Roger. I've got to meet my grandmother." She waved him off. "Call me later."

As she neared the main building, she saw a crowd gathered near the gravel drive that curved in front of it. Quickening her pace, she soon saw her grandmother's Bentley. Parked in front of it was a bright red sports car.

Regina Ryan was standing beside the Bentley, and as Caitlin went toward her, she smiled and extended her arms.

"So here you are." She spoke in a voice that easily carried to the students standing on the lawns. "How are you?" She extended her cheek for Caitlin's kiss.

"I'm fine, Grandmother." Confused by her grandmother's unexpected display of affection, Caitlin still managed a smile. "I was surprised to get your message."

"I had a few free hours and thought I would stop by." Mrs. Ryan looked conspiratorially across to Rollins standing on the other side of the Bentley. The driver grinned.

Caitlin was puzzled. What was her grandmother up to?

Regina laid a hand on her granddaughter's arm. "I have a little surprise for you, actually. You know we won't be going off on our usual trip this summer, and you'll be a senior next year. You will need to be more independent." She began walking

Caitlin toward the red car in front of the Bentley. "What do you think of it?" Regina motioned to the Nissan 280 ZX.

Frowning, Caitlin cast her grandmother a curious look. "It's nice—" she began.

Before she could say another word, Regina withdrew a silver keychain from her pocket and held it in front of Caitlin. "And all yours. Here are the keys."

"Mine?" Caitlin stared with wide eyes at the luxurious sports car. She couldn't believe it. Her grandmother was giving her a car? She looked at the keys her grandmother still held, then looked at her grandmother's face.

Regina nodded and smiled.

Caitlin slowly accepted the keys. "I don't know what to say. Thank you! I'm so surprised!"

"Go sit behind the wheel," Regina encouraged.

Caitlin stepped around the back of the car, well aware of the stares of the students gathered on the lawn. Why had her grandmother done this? Why here at school? What point was she trying to make? Caitlin was mystified. Yet whatever her grandmother's reasons, Caitlin had to admit it was an incredible piece of showmanship on her part.

Caitlin opened the door of the low-slung car and gracefully slid onto the white leather seat. What a feeling, just sitting behind the wheel! She could picture herself whirling over the country roads, the tape deck playing her favorite songs. How free she'd be!

Her eyes dazed and dreamy, she looked out to see Jed emerging from the crowd. Immediately she hopped out of the car, happy to see him. She wanted him to share her excitement.

Jed had gone first to Mrs. Ryan and was shaking her hand as Caitlin hurried toward them. She heard the end of their conversation.

". . . a little surprise for my granddaughter . . . time she had a car of her own."

"Jed! Isn't it incredible! Do you like it? Come and see!"

Caitlin missed her grandmother's frown as she led Jed away.

He was grinning and shaking his head. "Your grandmother sure is full of little tricks, isn't she?" he said in an undertone.

"Tricks? What do you mean?"

"Never mind. This isn't the place to talk about it." He ran his hand over the gleaming paint and bent over to look inside. "Nice, real nice. Are you still going to talk to me?"

"Oh, Jed, don't be silly! Do you think this car would make any difference between us?"

"Just teasing. Are you going to take it out for a ride, or do you have to get to the Fosters'?"

"Ian! Oh, no! I was so excited, I totally forgot, and I'm late. Let me go talk to my grandmother."

But Mrs. Ryan was already walking toward them. She was smiling again.

"Grandmother, I have to go," Caitlin explained in a rush. "I'm supposed to be at the Fosters' at three-thirty."

"Not today, dear. I've already spoken to the dean, and they've made other arrangements. In fact, I suggested to him that, considering your

36

workload, perhaps he should make other plans for the last week of school."

Caitlin stared at her grandmother in disbelief. What business of hers was it what Caitlin did with her time at Highgate?

Mrs. Ryan continued speaking as though she noticed nothing unusual. "Of course, Dean Foster informs me that Ian will be going off to a special school for the summer."

"He will?"

"Yes. Haven't the Fosters told you?"

"No."

"They're doing the right thing, getting him the care he needs." Mrs. Ryan lightly placed her hand on her granddaughter's shoulder. "Now, why don't you take a drive in your new car? Get in." She was holding the door open for Caitlin. "Rollins, ride with her this time and see how your student has progressed."

Caitlin had received her driver's license that spring, thanks to Rollins's coaching, but she hadn't done any driving on her own since then. She knew her grandmother was only being cautious in sending the chauffeur along. But if anyone should have been going along on this trial ride, it should have been Jed.

She started to call out to him.

Quickly he shook his head. "I'll talk to you later, Caitlin."

Nodding, Caitlin inserted the key in the ignition, and the engine roared to life. As she shifted into first gear, she glanced at Rollins.

He smiled. "Easy on the clutch, and you'll do just fine."

Concentrating on coordinating the clutch and the gas pedal, and afraid she'd make a mistake in front of her grandmother, Caitlin was almost amazed as the car began to move smoothly away from the curb.

"Good." Rollins beamed. "Now a little more gas."

As they rolled away down the Highgate drive under a canopy of oaks, Caitlin still felt dazed. She needed time to think. Her grandmother had dropped so many surprises in her lap so quickly—this car . . . and Ian. She found it hard to believe she wouldn't be working with the little boy anymore or that the Fosters hadn't told her they were sending Ian away.

Despite the excitement and exhilaration of driving the car, she couldn't wait to get back to the campus and talk to Jed. He would know what to do, and she'd feel so much better just sharing her confusion with him.

"I could be all wrong, but I think she's bribing you, Caitlin," Jed said later that evening. They were sitting in the main lounge in her dormitory.

"But why?" she wondered.

"To keep you in Virginia, for starters."

"She still hasn't given me her answer about Montana," Caitlin noted.

"Maybe she has. Maybe it's the car. Why else would she give it to you now? You certainly wouldn't get much use out of it if you were two thousand miles away."

"She did say we were getting too close," Caitlin mused. "But why would she want to stop me from helping Ian?" Caitlin actually knew the answer but needed confirmation.

"Maybe it doesn't fit in with her plans for you."

Caitlin slumped down in the couch. "There's no 'maybe' about it. Grandmother has this thing about volunteer work. Oh, it's okay to raise money for organizations that help others, but to actually do the work . . ." Caitlin wrinkled her nose in disgust. "Still, this is the dean's son. I thought that'd make a difference."

"Obviously not, I'm afraid." Jed patted her reassuringly on the shoulder. "But it's only a week, and if you'd gone to Montana you wouldn't be seeing him anymore anyway."

"Poor Ian." Caitlin sighed. "He really looked forward to my visits. I hope he's not hurt."

"Won't your grandmother even let you say good-bye to him? I can't believe she'd be that cold."

"Oh, when she's pressed she can be as cold as the North Pole," Caitlin snapped. "But she didn't say I couldn't see him at all. You're right, Jed. I'll go over there in the morning."

Saturday morning Dean Foster was out in the yard, trimming the grass, when Caitlin arrived.

"Well, hello there, Caitlin," he called in his usual friendly way. "You've come to see Ian?"

"Yes. Am I too early?"

"No, go on in. He's inside."

Caitlin let herself in the front door and peeked into the living room. Ian was there in his wheelchair drawing away.

"Hi, Ian."

The little boy looked up. "Caitlin! I missed you yesterday," he cried eagerly.

"I missed you, too."

"Where were you?"

"My grandmother was here at the school, and I had to see her."

"That's okay then."

She walked over to his wheelchair and knelt down beside him. "What have you been drawing?"

"Animals from the African book you gave me."

"Wow, these are good! Have you shown your mother and father?"

"Yup. We put some on the refrigerator."

"I thought I heard voices in here. Hello, Caitlin." Elaine Foster stepped around from the kitchen.

"Oh, hi, Mrs. Foster." Caitlin smiled. "Since I didn't see Ian yesterday, I thought I'd stop by and say hi."

"That's nice of you. I just took a batch of cookies out of the oven. Why don't you come into the kitchen with me and fill a plate for you and Ian."

Caitlin understood the unsaid message; Mrs. Foster wanted to talk to her alone. Once they were in the kitchen, she motioned Caitlin over to the stove at the far side of the room.

"I was sorry to hear you won't be able to sit with

Ian in the afternoons anymore. Dean Foster and I can't thank you enough for all you've done for him." Mrs. Foster took a spatula and began taking the chocolate-chip cookies off the tray and putting them on a plate.

"I've really liked doing it, Mrs. Foster, and if you haven't already made other arrangements, I'd like to come over a few days next week. I guess my grandmother was worried about my schedule and told Dean Foster it might be too much for me."

"I'm not surprised she was worried. You *have* been spending a lot of time here."

Caitlin glanced down at her hands. "My grandmother said that Ian's going off to a special school. I was so surprised—"

"We only found out ourselves yesterday morning that he'd been accepted," Mrs. Foster said, a little sheepishly. "You know we would have told you, Caitlin."

"I'll miss him."

"And I know he'll miss you, too. It's going to be hard explaining to him why he has to leave home for the summer and won't be seeing you anymore."

"Would it help if I talked to him?"

"It might help a lot." Mrs. Foster handed her the plate of cookies. "Why don't you take these in? I'll get a glass of milk for Ian. Would you like one, too?"

"No, thanks." Caitlin hesitated. "Would you mind giving me his address at the school? I'd like to write him this summer."

"Not at all. I think that would be a wonderful

idea. We're hoping he'll make enough progress over the summer so that he can come home in September."

"I hope so, too."

By the time Caitlin left the Fosters' an hour later, she felt much better. The knowledge that she'd be able to stay in touch with Ian over the summer eased some of the anxiety she'd been feeling. She had to help Ian walk again. It was important—so very, very important.

5

"This is totally amazing! How could I have collected so much junk this year?" Caitlin threw up her hands as she stared at the piles of books and papers she'd just taken out of the bookcase. "I've already run out of boxes."

Ginny chuckled from the other side of the room, where she was doing her own share of packing. "Guess we're just going to have to start throwing things out. My mother'll have a fit if I come home with all this. I don't even know if Daddy can fit it in the wagon."

Caitlin pulled her long hair away from her face and twisted it at the back of her neck. With their final exams now out of the way, they'd set aside that Thursday afternoon for packing. Since both of them hated the job so much, they were determined to get it out of the way as quickly as possible.

"We still have another two days before we have to move out of here," Ginny added, "if that's any consolation."

Caitlin stared at the boxes around her in disgust.

"Yuck! Why didn't you keep after me not to be such a packrat?"

"You keep everything so neat, I never even noticed. Now, on my side of the room, it's pretty obvious what wasn't here at the beginning of the year." Ginny dragged another cardboard box into the corner where it would wait until her parents arrived on Saturday. "When are you taking Duster home?"

"Tomorrow," Caitlin said distractedly as she made a concerted effort to slip a few more books into an already overcrowded box. "Jeff's bringing over the trailer. What about Cinnamon?"

"I'm boarding him for the summer. He's being picked up on Saturday. When's Jed coming?"

"He should be here in a few minutes." Caitlin placed her hands on her hips and looked around her. "Maybe I ought to start taking some of this down to the car."

"And where are you going to put all that stuff?"

"In the trunk. It's got a lot more space than you'd think. It's really great having the car, not having to rely on Rollins to lug all this junk for me."

"Sure, you've got Jed to do it now," Ginny observed.

"Ginny Brookes, that's not fair!" Caitlin cried. She brandished one of her books in the air as if ready to throw it at her friend.

Ginny pretended to take cover behind a cardboard box. "Hey, only kidding," she pleaded. "You driving home this afternoon?"

"I don't want to have to be moving all of it tomorrow, with the prom and all. Besides, it's a gorgeous day for a ride."

44

Caitlin turned and lifted up one of the cardboard boxes. "Can you get the door for me?" she called to her roommate.

Ginny swung the door wide, and Caitlin slipped through the doorway and then went slowly down the stairs. She'd brought her car around to the student parking lot behind the dorm, so she didn't have much of a trek.

Still, she was relieved to be able to set down her burden on the pavement. She reached into her pocket for the keys, unlocked the trunk, then picked up the box and shoved it way in the back. Leaving the trunk open, she headed toward the dorm for another load.

She'd made four trips by the time Jed came walking down the path leading from his dorm. She was just about to put another box in the trunk when she saw him.

"It's about time you got here—now that all the work is done!" she chided. But she was grinning. Jed had his own packing to do, and she really hadn't expected him earlier.

He came up to her and gave her a quick hug and kiss. "You must have left something for me to do."

"Yeah, I did. There're two more boxes."

"I'll go get them. I don't think Mrs. Chaney will mind my going upstairs if it's just to help you move."

"Of course she won't. I'll organize the trunk while you're gone."

Before lifting the last box into the trunk, Caitlin leaned over and pushed the other boxes around so that there wasn't an inch of space wasted. She heaved that box in, then turned to inspect her work just as Jed was coming down the path with his own burden.

Out of the corner of her eye, she noticed lying on the pavement a slim book that had fallen from one of her overstuffed boxes. Immediately she recognized the cover—her favorite book of love poems—and a chill went through her body. Quickly she leaned down to pick it up and turned just as Jed reached the back of the car.

"Okay." He sighed. "This definitely is *it* from the looks of this trunk."

As he fitted in the last two boxes, Caitlin went to the side of the car, opened the glove compartment, and dropped in the poetry book. Her heart was beating rapidly. It wasn't a book she wanted Jed to see just yet.

Jed slammed the trunk closed. "Ready to go?" he called.

"Sure am!" She was smiling brightly as she met him at the back of the car. "You want to drive?"

He shook his head. "I don't want to take any chances with this car. Your grandmother . . ."

"I know." Caitlin winked. "Well, get in. Let's go!"

Caitlin drove the first ten miles to Ryan Acres with less caution than could have been expected from a still-inexperienced driver. At one point she nearly ran a light, going through the intersection just as it changed from amber to red. Jed said nothing but gave her a raised-eyebrow look.

"Well, at least I'm not speeding." Caitlin looked back at him under her lashes. She was loving every minute of the ride, relishing the freedom, and enjoying the sight of Jed in the seat next to her.

"I didn't say anything." He smiled. "But I was just thinking. Brett Perkins wanted to know if we could give anyone a ride over to the lake after the prom tomorrow. Now I'm not so sure."

"Well, maybe we could squeeze one person in," Caitlin said skeptically. "But that wouldn't do much good, would it?"

He shook his head. "Let Brett figure out the transportation. It's his party."

Caitlin reached over and took Jed's hand. "I can't wait until tomorrow. It's going to be so much fun."

Jed smiled. "It better be—it'll be our last night together for a while."

"I'm going to talk to my grandmother again Saturday. Maybe she'll surprise us both and say I can go." She tried to sound optimistic, but both she and Jed—without really saying so in words—had resigned themselves to spending the summer apart.

"In any event, my plane leaves Saturday afternoon. My uncle will be picking me up in the morning."

"You're sure you don't want me to take you?"

"It'll be their only chance to see me. And they've been very good to me this year. Besides, I hate airport good-byes," Jed said.

Caitlin nodded, turned to smile at him quickly, then looked forward again. "Gosh, I should get gas."

"There's a station up the road." Jed pointed.

Caitlin saw the Exxon sign up ahead and carefully pulled in next to the pumps. It was her first gas fill, and she was a little nervous.

"Fill it up," she called to the attendant when he approached the car. "Credit card," she added, trying to act more assured. She turned to Jed. "I'll be right back. I want to go to the ladies' room."

Jed nodded.

The car's tank was small, and it was only a matter of minutes before the attendant came to Jed's window. "That'll be eleven-eighty."

Jed glanced toward the station. No sign of Caitlin yet.

"Maybe she's got the card in here." He reached in the glove compartment and drew out the book of poems so he could get a better look. No sign of a card. "You'll have to wait until she gets back. No, on second thought, let me get it."

As he reached in his back pocket for his wallet, the book of poems fell off his lap, and a folded letter slid out from between the pages. Jed handed the attendant twelve dollars, then reached on the floor to retrieve the paper. The letter had come unfolded, and as he picked it up, he couldn't miss reading his name at the top or notice that it had been dated months before.

"Jed," he read. "You know how very, very much I love you, but there's something I have to tell you. I'm ashamed that I haven't said this sooner . . ."

The last sentence surprised him. He knew he shouldn't be reading the letter, even if it was addressed to him. It was Caitlin's private property. But curiosity had gotten the better of him. What was Caitlin too ashamed of to tell him? Why had she written the letter months earlier and never given it to him? His eyes were drawn back to the letter almost against his will: "but it's been so wonderful to have you come into my life. I was afraid to tell you the truth because I might lose you."

Nervously he glanced up and saw Caitlin approaching from around the side of the station building. Quickly he folded the letter and thrust it in his back pocket, then slipped the book of poetry back into the glove compartment and snapped it shut.

He felt guilty as Caitlin gave him a big smile, but it was too late. The letter was already in his pocket.

"Where did the station guy go? I've got to pay him." Caitlin dug into her bag for her wallet.

"I took care of it."

"You didn't have to do that."

"It was only twelve dollars."

"Thanks." Her eyes were soft when she looked at him. "But it would have gone on my grand-mother's credit card."

"That's okay."

Jed was quiet during the rest of the ride, but Caitlin was in such an elated mood she didn't notice his single-syllable replies as she chattered on about the prom and the party and what she would say to her grandmother about their summer plans.

When they reached Ryan Acres, Rollins came to meet them at the door. "We weren't expecting you today, Miss Ryan," he said with pleased surprise.

"I thought I'd start bringing home some of my

books. It'll make it easier for you this weekend. We've got a trunkful."

As Caitlin started to the back of the car to open the trunk, Jed got out on his side. "Hi, there, Rollins."

"Hello, Jed. Good to see you."

"I'll help you carry these in," Jed offered. "Where do you want them, Caitlin?"

"In the storage room for now, I guess. I'll only have to bring them all back to Highgate in September."

Caitlin grabbed a carton herself and followed the two men into the house and down the hall to the storage room in the servants' wing.

"We'll get the rest, Miss Ryan," Rollins told her.

"Okay, if you don't mind." She brushed off her hands on her jeans. "I just want to run upstairs, Jed. There's some jewelry in my room that would look great with my dress tomorrow."

"Sure, take your time."

In one more trip Jed and Rollins had the car unpacked. Caitlin hadn't returned from her room yet, and as Jed went back in the house, he felt as if the letter were burning a hole in his pocket.

"I'm just going to wash my hands," he told Rollins. "If Caitlin comes down, tell her I'll be right back."

He went into the guest bathroom at the end of the hall and closed and locked the door behind him. He was torn between giving in to his curiosity and reading the letter, or slipping it back into the book of poetry, unread, while Caitlin was still upstairs. He had to know what Caitlin was so ashamed of, and why she was so afraid she'd lose him. It was probably something silly, but he still felt compelled to find out. He withdrew the letter from his pocket and unfolded it, starting to read where he'd left off.

. . . I was afraid to tell you the truth because I might lose you.

I've just come back from talking to Emily. She told me that Diana's left the school she'd just transferred to. I feel responsible.

It goes back to the accident at the Fosters' when Ian got into the poison. I was there that day. I went to the shed to get a prop for the fund-raiser. The door was locked. I remembered having to unlock it and then hanging the key back up. But when I came out, I'd forgotten all about it being locked. I was tired and aggravated, and I kicked the door shut behind me. Ian was in the yard, but he didn't see me leaving.

It's true I hated Diana for getting you when I couldn't. It's true I did everything in my power to get you away from her. But I didn't deliberately leave that shed door unlocked. I never would have done anything like that! I just didn't think to lock it again. It was a terrible oversight.

I went back to the auditorium, where I heard the ambulance and learned that Ian had been hurt. I blamed Diana. I thought she'd been inside the house with you all that time. Besides, I was angry that everyone felt so sorry for her. I couldn't understand what it was she had that made her so well liked. I didn't tell anyone that I'd been in the Fosters' yard that day and knew she'd taken her eyes off Ian. I didn't tell anyone because I was almost sure you'd been in the house with her, and I didn't want to implicate you.

I didn't find out what really happened and learn about the poisoning until the following weekend. I was at my grandmother's, and the story was on the front page of the paper.

Once I read the article, I knew I was really to blame. I ran out of the house, got on one of the horses, and took a long ride in the pouring rain. I couldn't face the truth or admit it to myself. I wanted to die. Instead, I got sick and spent the next week in bed. I couldn't let myself think about it. It hurt too much.

By the time I came back to school, Diana was gone for good. I thought everything would blow over. I felt weak and tired, and I still couldn't face the truth. I told myself Diana would find a new life—a good life—away from Highgate. I even avoided you because you were a reminder of the horrible secret I was keeping. Then you came to talk to me at the party. When you said you'd misjudged me, I didn't have the courage to tell you what I'd really done. I'd wanted you for so long, I just couldn't say the words.

Oh, Jed, I feel so terrible for lying to you. I want your love and respect, and I want us to stay together, but the only way I can live with myself is to tell you this. I can't stand these feelings of guilt any longer.

I know I am responsible for a lot of unhappiness and have a great debt to pay, but please tell me you'll forgive me. Please tell me you still love me!

I love you,
Caitlin

Jed's hands were shaking when he'd finished reading. All this time, Caitlin had been lying to him—hiding the truth—while Diana had been suffering needlessly! Emily had told him only a few days before that Diana was now in the hospital. And all the while it had been Caitlin who'd been to blame for Ian's poisoning! Caitlin was responsible for Diana's condition!

And the worst was that she'd *deliberately* deceived him and the entire school. All these months since the accident, since they'd been going together, she'd let him believe that she was innocent, that she was helping Ian as an act of genuine unselfishness. Unselfishness? She'd been acting out of guilt! She'd held on to Jed's love—and Ian's affection—through false pretenses!

Jed was so angry he could barely breathe. Caitlin had written him this letter, true, but then she'd obviously decided not to give it to him. The fact that it was in the glove compartment of her new car made him wonder if she'd changed her mind and decided to tell him the truth after all. But even that thought didn't soften his anger—not when Caitlin had callously allowed Diana to suffer for so long!

What a *fool* he was! He should have known she couldn't have changed much from the Caitlin he'd first met when he'd transferred to Highgate the previous fall. He'd decided then that she was no more than a flirt—and a spoiled one at that—used to getting her own way by using people. She'd always had three or four guys hanging around her, and he'd seen how she played one against the other.

How could he have forgotten how Caitlin had tried to break him and Diana up, especially during that weekend party she'd had at Ryan Acres? She'd done everything she could then to make Diana feel miserable and out of place and keep the two of them apart. At the time, Jed thought maybe he'd been imagining things. Caitlin had seemed so hurt when he'd suggested that she was deliberately being mean to Diana. Now he saw that she'd been manipulating him and everyone else at the party!

But then Caitlin had seemed to change. She'd been sick and missed a couple of weeks of school, he remembered, and when she'd returned to Highgate, she'd seemed so different—so quiet, not the party girl anymore. But of course—that had been *after* Ian's accident, *after* Diana had left Highgate! Caitlin's sudden sweetness had been an act, too! Either that, or she'd actually been feeling a few pangs of well-deserved guilt—although not enough to confess to what she'd done.

Damn! Jed nearly pounded his fist into the bathroom wall. How foolish he'd been! He'd really believed she'd changed—he'd really believed that the new Caitlin was the real Caitlin, and he'd let himself fall in love with her. Instead, the *real* Caitlin was the opportunist who'd resort to any means to get what she wanted, including destroying the life and happiness of an innocent girl. How Caitlin must have gloated to see Diana leave the school and have her only adversary out of the way once and for all!

He wanted to kill her! He wanted to kill himself

for being taken in and playing right into her hands. How could he have been so stupid as to fall in love with her?

What was he to do? His instincts told him to confront her with it and tell her exactly what he thought of her deceit, lies, and selfishness!

But his emotions said no, that wouldn't be enough punishment for her. Caitlin should have to suffer, too! He'd have to take another course of action.

He refolded the letter and left the bathroom. Caitlin was still nowhere in sight, so he went out to the front drive. Reaching into the car, he opened the glove compartment and slid the letter back into the book of poetry. Then he straightened up and went back into the house.

Caitlin was just coming down the hall.

"There you are!" she called happily. "I just asked Catherine to fix us a snack. You must be hungry by now."

Jed shook his head. "No, we should head back soon. I've got a lot of stuff to do at the dorm tonight."

Caitlin linked her arm through his as they walked down the hall. "You're not coming over tonight?"

"I've got to pack, too, you know," he said.

"But I'll have you all to myself tomorrow night," she teased.

"Right," Jed said tersely. He wanted Caitlin to think that nothing had changed, that the prom would be their final farewell for the year, a night for both of them to remember all summer long.

Jed would make sure Caitlin remembered, but if everything went according to his plan, it would end up being a night she would much rather forget.

6

"Wow!" Ginny exclaimed as she helped Caitlin into her prom gown, carefully buttoning the silk-covered buttons that ran up the back of the luxurious garment. "It's magnificent. You look like you just came from Versailles."

"Thanks, old buddy." Caitlin grinned. "That's exactly what I told my grandmother when I tried it on in Paris last summer. She thought it was too sophisticated for a girl my age, but I managed to convince her that all the *belles femmes* of the eighteenth century wore dresses like this."

Caitlin felt she had every right to be proud of her purchase. The pure silk dress in soft violet had a scooped neck and puffed sleeves that ended in a row of buttons at her wrists. The fitted waist and long, flared skirt were most flattering to her slim five-foot, eight-inch body. Earlier in the day, Caitlin had pulled her long, dark hair into a mass of ringlets on top of her head and had polished her nails a soft pink. She couldn't wait for Jed to see her.

She turned to her roommate. "You look pretty,

yourself. This has got to be the first time I've seen you in a dress in months."

"Yeah," Ginny agreed, straightening the skirt of her much simpler flowered toile gown. "Long dresses aren't exactly me, but I can't go to the prom dressed in jodhpurs."

Caitlin laughed. "Come on, Ginny, can't you admit it's fun to get dressed up like this?"

"Well, maybe. Anyway, it's about time Bert saw me in a dress."

"Believe me, he won't be disappointed."

"Neither will Jed."

"I hope you're right, Ginny. Tonight's very important to me." Caitlin glowed as she glided to her jewelry box. She reached inside for her antique amethyst necklace and matching drop earrings. After she put them on, she took out a long strand of pearls. "Here, Ginny, why don't you wear these tonight. They'll look great with your dress."

Before Ginny could respond, Caitlin had moved over and clasped the necklace around her friend's neck. Then she turned Ginny to face the mirror. "Perfect," she said.

"Thanks, Caitlin!"

"My pleasure." Caitlin was feeling wonderful, full of expectation for what was shaping up as one of the best nights of her life. Easing Ginny away from the mirror, she added a final touch of blusher to her cheeks and applied a deep plum shade of lipstick to her lips.

When she was finished, Caitlin opened the closet door and inspected herself in the full-length mirror on the back. She repositioned one of the combs holding up her hair so that several tendrils fell freely to the side, creating a slightly softer look. "I'm ready when you are," she said, satisfied she looked as appealing as she could.

Ginny stuffed a comb and lipstick into her evening bag and picked up her white fox jacket off the bed. "Let's go."

Caitlin took her own beaded bag off the dresser, wrapped her black sable wrap around her shoulders, and followed Ginny down to the lounge.

Caitlin put on one of her prettiest smiles as she entered the room, expecting to see Jed sitting on one of the couches. But he wasn't there.

Bert Simpson, Ginny's boyfriend, was one of the small group of boys there, and he rose quickly as soon as he saw the girls. "Hi, Ginny, Caitlin." The tall, lanky boy looked rather uncomfortable in his black tuxedo. "You look pretty tonight, Ginny."

A blush rose on Ginny's cheeks. "Thanks," she whispered.

"Have you seen Jed?" Caitlin asked.

"No," Bert answered, "but it's still early."

"Yeah, he's probably on his way right now," Caitlin said lightly.

"You want us to wait?" Ginny asked.

"No, go on ahead. I'll see you inside."

Caitlin waved them off, but as soon as they were gone, a tiny frown appeared on her brow. She was concerned. Jed was *never* late. Could something have happened to him?

Caitlin put her smile back on when Tim Collins came in a moment later. They chatted amiably while he waited for his date, Gloria, to come downstairs.

She kept the smile up as first Roger and Morgan then Brett and Dorothy, Emily and Terry, and most of her other friends came and left. With each passing second, her worry deepened. Jed would never leave her waiting like this. Something must have happened to him.

Tired of pacing the long, narrow room, she leaned against the far wall, taking pains not to crease her dress. The dorm was frighteningly silent. Even Mrs. Chaney was gone, already fulfilling her duty as one of the prom's chaperons. Caitlin bit her lip, vowing not to let the tears that were welling up in her eyes fall.

Finally, several agonizing minutes later, the front door banged closed, Caitlin heard the sound of footsteps approaching the lounge.

She looked up, her prettiest smile back on her face. Despite her anger and worry, Caitlin sighed in appreciation when she saw Jed. He looked so handsome and appealing in his tuxedo that she silently forgave him for his lateness. She took a step forward to greet him, but for a moment he continued to stand in the doorway and stare at her.

His look made Caitlin feel uncomfortable. It was as if he saw something that displeased him. Caitlin had received too many compliments to believe it had anything to do with the way she looked. She wondered what could be bothering him.

A moment later he let his face relax and moved toward her. "You ready, Caitlin?"

"Yes, and I have been for the last half hour!" The words came out more sharply than she had intended.

"Let's go, then." Jed ignored her angry tone and headed toward the door, making Caitlin step up her pace to catch up to him.

Caitlin was not only irritated, but confused. It was unlike Jed to be so abrupt. He hadn't bothered to tell her how nice she looked or to give her his usual hug or to explain why he was so late.

They began to walk across campus to the gym, Caitlin hurrying to keep up with Jed's quick pace. "What happened," she asked.

He looked back at her. "What makes you think something happened?"

"Where were you? Everyone else is already at the gym. Why were you so late?"

"Was I late?" Jed said mockingly. "Don't worry. They wouldn't dare start the prom without you."

"What do you mean by that?" Caitlin asked. His strange attitude was making her uneasy.

Jed didn't answer.

They arrived at the gym. The double doors were wide open, letting the soft yellow glow of the indoor spotlights and the lilting music of the dance orchestra spill out into the mild June night. Caitlin wanted to press Jed for a response, but there were too many people around them now, their conversation filling the air.

"What a gorgeous night for a prom!"

"Doesn't the band sound wonderful?"

"Wonderful? This music was old when our parents were our age."

"The gym looks beautiful."

"Yeah, the decorating committee did a terrific job."

"Hey, Caitlin, you look great," said Matt Jenks, Jed's roommate. His smile was genuine, and he took Caitlin's hand and squeezed it in a gentle greeting.

Well, Caitlin thought. At least someone appreciated how good she looked—even if Jed hadn't bothered to compliment her. "Thanks, Matt," she replied. "Where's Mary?"

"Over at our table. Say, will you promise to dance with me later?"

"With pleasure," Caitlin said, turning to Jed as she spoke. His face was expressionless; she couldn't tell what he was thinking. "See you later."

Caitlin followed Jed to the reception table, where they checked in and cast their ballots for prom king and queen. They were met there by two underclassmen, also in formal wear, who led them to their assigned table.

The circular tables formed a U around the gym, with the traditional twelve-piece orchestra set up at the far end of the room. Next to the musicians were two high-backed chairs, reserved for the prom king and queen. Long drapes of deep blue cloth hid the basketball hoops and other gym equipment from view and gave the room an intimate feeling, which was heightened by the soft glow of candlelight from each of the tables. Baskets of flowers also sat on the tables, along with fine china, silver tableware, and crystal goblets.

Emily and Terry were already seated. "Let's sit right here," Jed said, taking a seat next to his cousin. He didn't bother to pull out the velvet-upholstered chair for Caitlin, but she hid her feelings as she sat herself down.

Caitlin was happy to be near Emily. Maybe she knew what was bothering Jed. "You look beautiful, Emily," Caitlin said.

Emily was wearing a dramatic white strapless chiffon gown. "You should talk," Emily bubbled. "As usual, you're the standout here."

"Did Emily tell you her good news?" Terry cut in. When Caitlin answered with a puzzled look, he went on. "Emily's been accepted into the Hunterson program!"

"Congratulations, Emily," Caitlin said. "But I still don't understand why you'd want to spend the summer in school."

"It's one of the most prestigious summer science programs in the country. It'll give me a head start for applying to colleges."

"Come on, Emily. With your grades you'll be able to get in anywhere," Caitlin said.

"Believe me, Hunterson won't hurt. And besides," she added, smiling impishly, "Hunterson's just five miles from Terry's place. We'll be able to see each other all summer."

"I'm happy for you," Caitlin said, her own insides churning.

Jed nodded. "It's too bad I can't be with Caitlin this summer. It doesn't look as if her grandmother will let her come out to the ranch, does it, Caitlin?"

"Well, I still haven't given up hope," she said, feeling terribly confused. Did this mean Jed wasn't mad at her, as she'd imagined? If not, then why was he acting so strangely?

Yet Caitlin would have thought nothing was wrong from the way Jed acted at the table. He joked with the others and shared horror stories about cramming for final exams.

The dance floor was filling with couples slow dancing to old love songs. Some of her classmates had hoped that Caitlin would have selected a rock band to play, but she had insisted on hiring the orchestra that had played at every Highgate prom for as long as anyone could remember. She had looked forward to an evening of dancing in Jed's arms, of having him hold her closely and tenderly as they danced to the old romantic songs.

One by one, the couples at her table got up to dance. Jed seemed in no hurry to rise until, it seemed to Caitlin, he realized they'd be the only couple left there. She really didn't mind staying seated because she hoped it would give them a chance to talk, but Jed didn't appear interested in being alone with her. "Let's go," he said, rising abruptly.

Caitlin felt as if Jed was only going through the motions as they danced. He felt stiff and very distant as they moved across the floor, and she thought she felt him pull back when she rested her head on his shoulder. She was relieved when the orchestra finished playing and the leader announced they were taking a break.

"I need some air. I'll meet you at the table," Jed said.

Confused, Caitlin returned to her seat. She smiled at Roger and Morgan and Brett and

Dorothy but ignored their chatter. She wasn't in the mood for party talk.

A few moments later she was joined by Emily and Terry. "Caitlin, this is fun. I've never been much of a dancer, but Terry's a wonderful teacher. I'm having a great time!" Emily paused when she noticed her friend's glum expression. "What's wrong?"

Immediately Caitlin put a smile on her face; she didn't want anyone to know how she was feeling. "Nothing," she said. Then thinking better of it she broached the subject with Emily. "Have you noticed anything wrong with Jed?"

"He looks fine to me. What's the matter?"

"I don't know. Something's bothering him, but he won't tell me what it is."

Emily shrugged. "He hasn't told me anything," she said. "But from what he said before, it sounds as if he's given up on your visiting him this summer. Maybe that's what's bothering him. To-night *is* your last night together."

"You don't have to remind me about that," Caitlin said. "Maybe I'm just overreacting. I just wanted everything to go perfectly tonight." She looked up. "Oh, here he comes. Well, speak of the devil," Caitlin said, smiling brightly again.

"Talking about me behind my back, eh?" Jed asked. "What deep, dark secrets has she been spilling, Emily?"

"Nothing you're unaware of," Emily said, not realizing how close to the truth her words were.

"I guess you're right, Emily," Jed said. "Caitlin's

not the type to keep secrets anyway, are you, Caitlin?"

"Oh, no," she said. Jed's words were making her very nervous.

"I didn't think so," he said.

Their conversation was cut short with the arrival of their dinner. Red-jacketed waiters in white shirts and black bow ties carried huge silver platters to each table, serving everyone plates of broiled steak, potatoes au gratin, and steamed vegetables.

"Good food, Caitlin," Roger said. "Glad you chose this caterer."

"She's the best in Virginia," Caitlin said proudly.

The orchestra came back and began to play quiet dinner music. Caitlin forced herself to eat, but with her confusion over Jed's behavior, she didn't enjoy it much. She was relieved, however, that the meal kept conversation down to a minimum.

As the waiters were removing their plates, Dean Foster approached the orchestra and motioned for them to stop playing. On noticing the dean, many at the tables began clinking their spoons against their water goblets, drawing their friends' attention to the podium.

"Thank you," Dean Foster said, quieting down the crowd. Once he was confident of everyone's attention, he continued.

"I hope you're all enjoying yourselves tonight. Your desserts will be served momentarily, but first I have an announcement to make. We've finished counting the ballots for prom king and queen. I'm going to announce the runners-up first. When I call your name, please walk out to the dance floor."

Dean Foster turned around to the band and nodded. The drummer began a drumroll. "Fourth runners-up: Tim Collins and Gloria Parks."

There were cheers from the crowd, and Tim gave them a mock bow as he walked onto the dance floor. An underclass attendant handed Gloria a long-stemmed rose.

Dean Foster continued. "Third runners-up: Jim Page and Kim Verdi." There was more applause as the couple rose from their table.

"Second runners-up: Brett Perkins and Dorothy Raite."

Caitlin tensed and looked at Jed expectantly. She was certain her name was one of the four going to be called. She so hoped she'd win.

"First runners-up: Roger Wake and Morgan Conway." Dean Foster waited until Morgan had received her rose before announcing the winners. "And our king and queen of the junior prom— come up here, Jed Michaels and Caitlin Ryan!"

The crowd went wild with applause. Caitlin let out a huge sigh, but her face was radiant. They'd won—just as she'd hoped. It couldn't be more perfect! Jed and she, king and queen.

One of the faculty came over to hand Caitlin a half-dozen roses, while one of the members of the prom committee brought forward the crowns. She could see Jed was embarrassed, but he smiled as he accepted the small crown. As the band started playing a processional march, Jed and Caitlin were led to the far end of the gym. There, they took their seats side by side and looked out over their "subjects."

After photographs had been taken for the yearbook and various classmates had come over to congratulate them, Jed and Caitlin were able to relax a little.

Jed leaned over to her. "Happy now?"

"Of course!" She was glowing with happiness. "Aren't you?"

He shrugged and gave her a long look. "It's different."

She was about to ask him what he meant, but some of the crowd had started shouting, "The king and queen should dance. The king and queen should dance!"

"Guess we'd better get up." Caitlin grinned, her worries about Jed momentarily forgotten with all the attention.

"They won't shut up if we don't," he agreed. "That's Roger egging them on."

As Caitlin and Jed took the floor, the crowd parted in a circle around them. They looked terrific, and Caitlin knew it. The louder the kids cheered, the wider she smiled. She was in her element. This was going to be a night to remember, after all.

7

It wasn't until an hour and a half later, when the orchestra had started to pack up and everyone was getting ready to leave, that Caitlin was again reminded of Jed's strange mood.

She was standing at the door with some of those who were going to Brett's party. "You all know the way," Brett was saying. "I've got my father's wagon. If you squeeze in, I can fit about eight. My father will be at the dock with the boat. The rest of you just head over to the lake. My father will keep coming back with the boat until he's picked up everyone and brought them to the island."

Jed had taken Caitlin's elbow. "Let's go."

He was quiet during the short walk to Caitlin's car.

"Are you tired?" she finally asked.

"No, not really."

"Do you want to drive?" She withdrew the keys from her bag as they reached the car.

"Yeah, maybe I will. You can't drive with that dress on anyway."

They both got in, and Jed started the car. He gunned the engine, then raced down the driveway and away from the school.

"Hey, take it easy," Caitlin said, alarmed.

"I know what I'm doing," Jed hissed.

During the short drive, Caitlin tried to convince herself that Jed's bad mood would pass. The more she thought about it, the more she felt Emily was right. School was almost over, and her grandmother still hadn't given her a definite answer about their summer plans. Jed was probably depressed about their not being able to see much of each other that summer.

Sure of herself, she reached over and lightly touched his leg. He jumped as if she'd pinched him.

"I didn't mean to scare you."

He relaxed. "I was just thinking."

"I can't believe this may be our last night together until fall." She sighed. "When I see my grandmother tomorrow, I'm going to make her give me an answer."

"Isn't that the road up on the right?" Jed said shortly.

Momentarily distracted, Caitlin glanced out the front window. "Must be. Brett said to look for a row of mailboxes."

Jed swung the car onto the short dirt drive that led to the shore of the lake. There was a small parking area near the dock, and he pulled the car in and turned off the engine. He handed Caitlin the keys. "Better keep those in your bag."

70

Caitlin wondered why Jed didn't just put the keys in his own pocket, but he was already out of the car. He came around to her side and helped her maneuver her full skirt out of the low-slung car. Several other cars pulled in right behind them, and in a minute the parking lot was full of people.

"Down this way," Brett called, leading them all to the wooden dock and the good-sized cabin cruiser that was tied up beside it. "Hi, Dad. Here's the first load. I won't introduce you to everyone. You'll never remember all the names."

"Hi, kids," Mr. Perkins greeted them. "Come on board. Watch your step, especially with those dresses."

Several of the girls, including Caitlin, had taken off their shoes for safety and held them in their hands as they climbed into the boat.

"Squeeze forward," Mr. Perkins instructed. "Go on down below. They're plenty of seats down there."

In the tight quarters, Caitlin was separated from Jed, but she wasn't concerned as she sat down with Ginny and Gloria.

"Wasn't the prom fabulous?" Gloria bubbled.

"I had a wonderful time," Caitlin said, hoping she sounded more enthusiastic than she felt.

"So did I. This party should be something, too! Brett says he bought lots of new records."

In a moment the engine started to hum, and Mr. Perkins drew the boat slowly away from the dock. The ride to the island only took a few minutes. Once the boat was secured, everyone filed off and followed Brett to the sprawling modern house set amid the trees on a rise above the lake. The house was surrounded by a huge illuminated deck.

As they gathered in the large living room off the deck, Caitlin walked over to Jed and linked her arm with his. "Nice place, isn't it?" she said looking around.

"Yeah, real nice," he said, sounding distracted. "Let's dance."

Brett had set up the stereo speakers so that they boomed out over the deck and could be heard over nearly the entire island. In a few minutes the deck was crowded with dancers. Jed and Caitlin stayed out there until both of them were nearly gasping for breath.

"I'm exhausted," Caitlin said, laughing. "I'm going to sit down for a minute. You feel like getting me a soda?"

As Jed headed toward the kitchen, Caitlin wandered into the living room, feeling better than she had all evening. Things were working out after all, she thought. The frenetic dancing seemed to have snapped Jed out of his mood. She wandered over to the center of the room, where a half dozen of her friends were grouped around the coffee table playing Trivial Pursuit.

"You guys should be out dancing," she teased.

"Not yet," Tim Collins answered. "Jim and I have a match going here. Throw the dice, Jim."

Jed came up with her soda as Jim was being read his question. "Thanks," she said, taking the glass from his hand. She nudged him and smiled secretly. "You want to play the next match?"

"No, I'm not in the mood for games tonight."
The way he looked at her with his eyes half-closed,
Caitlin was sure she understood his meaning. She
smiled at him and leaned a little closer against his
shoulder.

They watched the game for another few minutes, then Roger came up beside Caitlin. "Come
on, Caitlin. You still owe me a dance."

She looked at Jed in question.

He smiled. "Go ahead."

She followed Roger out to the deck and danced
with him for two songs. She was about to tell him
that she'd had enough when Terry came over and
cut in.

"I haven't danced with you in a long time," he
said as they started a slow dance.

No, not in months, Caitlin thought, not since the
fall when she and Terry had dated a few times.
How things had changed. Back then she would
never have thought of going out with only one boy
at a time, and Terry had been angry at her about
that.

"Congratulations on getting elected queen,"
Terry added. "I voted for you, you know."

"Gee, thanks, Terry." She grinned up at him. "I
won't tell Emily."

"That's okay, she knows. In fact, she insisted I
vote for you. She really thinks the world of you."

Caitlin glanced over Terry's shoulder and saw
Jed standing in the entrance to the living room,
watching her. In a moment he turned and went
back into the room. As soon as the dance was over,
Caitlin excused herself and followed after him.

He seemed perfectly happy when she reached his side. "Enjoy your dances?"

"Every now and again it's good to change partners," she teased.

"Let's go for a walk," he suggested.

Caitlin wasn't about to refuse a chance to be alone with him. "I'd love to," she said.

They left through the side door and began following one of the paths away from the house. It was wide and well cleared, and Caitlin had no trouble negotiating it with her long dress. Jed put his arm around her waist, and she leaned her head against his shoulder.

"This is better," he said. "It was getting too loud in there."

"I think I've had enough partying for one night," Caitlin agreed.

"But this one won't break up for another couple of hours."

"We could go home early."

"Why don't we just find a quiet place here." He drew his arm a little more tightly around her waist. "That looks like a building or something up ahead."

As they drew closer they saw that it was actually a small gazebo centered in a clearing in the trees.

Jed led her up the steps. There were cushions on the circular benches. The woods around them were quiet, and they were so far from the house they could barely hear the blaring music.

Caitlin sighed as they settled on one of the cushions.

74

"I've been waiting to get you alone all night," Jed said.

"You have?" she teased. "I wonder why." Then she added more seriously as she reached for his hand, "I thought there was something wrong before. You were so quiet."

"I guess I was." Jed drew his fingers gently down her cheek, rested them under her chin, and leaned toward her. In a moment his lips found hers, and he kissed her slowly.

Caitlin melted into his arms. All night long she'd felt so tense, but here at last was proof that Jed loved her. His kiss grew stronger. The hand that held her chin reached around her waist, and she lifted her own hand to tangle her fingers in his thick hair.

But instead of gently caressing her back as he'd always done before, his touch was much rougher, more insistent. He pulled her tightly against his chest as he trailed a stream of kisses down her neck to the edge of the bodice of her dress.

They'd been together like this before, but this time Caitlin sensed something different in Jed—an urgency that almost scared her.

But this was Jed, she told herself, her wonderful Jed. There was nothing to be afraid of. She *wanted* to enjoy his touch and his kisses.

His touch grew more daring.

His hand on her waist moved slowly upward. As his mouth recaptured hers, his hand reached the neckline of her gown.

"Oh!" she cried involuntarily against his mouth.

"Shhh," he whispered. "Let me touch you, Caitlin . . . let me. I love you so much."

His words were almost hypnotic. She couldn't deny the shivers of excitement that rippled through her body at his touch.

Caitlin felt her back arching and heard herself moan. Slowly, gradually, he leaned her back against the cushions. His hand drifted back down over her midriff, over her hip, and the skirt of her gown.

Again, Caitlin tried to protest, but again, he silenced her with his mouth as his hand began moving in gentle circles. She was trembling with the sensations he was bringing her. She wanted him to stop—yet something inside her wouldn't allow her to protest.

Sensing her resistance, he brought his lips up to her ear. "Caitlin, I love you. Let me show you. I've wanted to do this for so long."

"We can't, Jed. We can't."

"I'll be careful. Don't worry."

"No—I can't!"

"You love me, don't you?" he persisted.

"Oh, of course. Of course, I love you."

"We belong together . . . we always will. Between us it's good, it's beautiful."

"Oh, Jed, Jed," she cried.

He kissed her again, but this time his kiss was hard, violent. She felt as if he were bruising her mouth, and she tried to pull away.

"Stop, Jed. Stop!" She pressed her hands against his chest.

"Not now, Caitlin. Not now. I need you . . . I need you too much."

This isn't how it's supposed to be, something inside Caitlin cried. She'd dreamed of the day she'd finally give her love to Jed—but not like this!

He began kissing her neck, but his kisses were almost painful. "You're such a tease, Caitlin . . . such a tease," he murmured. She could barely hear him. Her heart was beating in panic. "You'd use anyone to get what you want, wouldn't you?"

No, she couldn't have heard him correctly. What was he talking about?

"Now, I'm going to use you."

"No! No, Jed. Stop! I don't want this! Please!"

"Why should I listen to you," he rasped. "You've spent your whole life taking advantage of others. It's about time someone took advantage of you."

Caitlin felt frozen. This couldn't be happening! This wasn't the Jed she knew.

Then suddenly he stopped, "No!" He cried suddenly, as if to himself. "No, I can't! I can't do it, even to you!" In one quick action, he flung himself away from her and turned.

Numb and beyond comprehension, Caitlin stared at him. "What is it? What have I done? Why are you doing this to me?"

He started walking away, out of the gazebo.

"Jed! Tell me what's wrong! Please!"

"If you don't know, Caitlin, I'm not going to tell you." And he kept walking.

"No, Jed. Come back!" She pushed herself to her

feet, started after him, but quickly realized she couldn't face the others yet. In defeat and embarrassment, she sat down on the bench and covered her face with her hands. Why, oh why? she sobbed uncontrollably. Why had he done this to her?

8

Caitlin didn't sleep at all that night, and even Ginny's sympathetic coaxings couldn't pull from her the truth of what had happened.

The rest of the night at the party had been a nightmare. After Jed left her, it had taken her many minutes to pull herself together and return to the house. She'd gone right to the bathroom to wash her tear-streaked face, recomb her hair, and make sure her dress was in place. She felt totally disoriented, as if she were in shock.

She didn't want to talk to anyone, and she waited in a darkened hallway until she saw Mr. Perkins in the kitchen alone and asked him if he'd give her a ride back across the lake.

The party was still in full swing. Caitlin had no idea whether Jed was still there or not, and at that moment she didn't care. She was so mad at him, so disbelieving that he could have been so callous and cold, that she never wanted to see him again.

She left the house through the side door after retrieving her bag and wrap from the bedroom and walked down to the dock to wait for Mr. Perkins.

He took her back in his small, motorized dinghy, and Caitlin was thankful she was the only passenger.

Her car was in the parking lot exactly where Jed had left it. Pulling her dress up to her knees she squeezed behind the driver's wheel and reached inside her bag for her keys. Now she knew why he'd given them to her. He'd deliberately planned the whole evening, and that realization only fueled her anger at him. How he'd fooled her all these months! Inside, the Jed Michaels she'd known had been a monster, one crueler and more despicable than anyone she'd ever known.

Not until she was in her own room did the finality of what had happened hit her. Her knees nearly buckled under her at the pain and humiliation she felt. Seeing the familiar room stripped of its personal touches only made her feel worse. *It's over, it's all over,* she realized. A terrible sense of emptiness engulfed her.

She collapsed on the bed, and as she sobbed she pounded her fists into the pillow. Why? She thought back over everything that had happened, everything that had been said during the whole horrendous evening. What had she done? What was it Jed had said as he'd walked away? "If you don't know, Caitlin, I'm not going to tell you."

There was only one thing she could think of that might have made him act the way he had, only one thing terrible enough to have made him change so completely. Her stomach clenched painfully at the thought. It was the only thing that made sense: He'd found out the truth. Somehow, some way, he'd discovered that she was responsible for the accident that had crippled Ian Foster. But how would he know that? Nobody knew the truth except her. Nobody.

Then she remembered the book of poems she'd put in the glove compartment of her car. He must have seen the letter that she'd written to him months before and been afraid to give him. But how would he have known it was there? Why would he have looked?

With an energy she didn't know she possessed, she ran out of the dorm and across the lawn to the parking lot. Her fingers trembled as she pressed open the glove compartment. She was almost afraid to feel inside. But the book was there, just as she'd left it. Heaving a hugh sigh, she took the book out and opened it. Even in the dim light in the parking lot, she could see that the letter was still inside.

Book in hand, she returned to her room. She wanted nothing more than to destroy the evidence forever. She unfolded the letter just to be sure. Yes, there were her own damning words. She ripped the letter to shreds, ran down the hall, and flushed the scraps down the toilet.

But she felt no better when she got back to the room. Destroying the letter had served no purpose except to vent her frustration. The memories of the last few hours came back to her, and she started to cry again.

Half in a daze, she got out of her dress and into her nightgown. Like a zombie, she went down the hall and brushed her teeth and splashed water over her hot cheeks. But she knew she wouldn't sleep. She was still sobbing when Ginny got home two hours later.

"Caitlin, are you all right?" Ginny asked, walking straight to Caitlin's bed. "I looked for you at the party, but you'd left. Mr. Perkins said he'd taken you across the lake alone. What happened? Where did Jed go?"

"I don't want to talk about it, Ginny," Caitlin said, sniffling.

"Come on. You'll probably feel better if you do. Did you two have a fight? You seemed to be having a good time."

"It was awful, Ginny. I don't want to talk about it."

"You had a fight?"

Caitlin only shook her head and buried her face in the pillow.

Ginny tried to persuade Caitlin to talk but finally gave up when Caitlin turned her face to the wall. "Don't be afraid to wake me up if you decide you need to talk," Ginny told her.

Caitlin dozed off from time to time, but by six in the morning she knew she couldn't lie in her bed a moment longer. Carefully, so as not to wake her still-sleeping friend, she got out some clothes and her cosmetic kit and slipped down the hall to shower and dress. When she saw herself in the mirror, she couldn't believe how swollen her eyes looked. She pressed a cold washcloth to them, then took a cool shower. Her body was so numb from lack of sleep, she barely felt the chill.

She put enough makeup on her face to hide the

signs of her crying, then went back to the room to drop off her nightgown and cosmetic kit. During her sleepless hours, she'd made up her mind about what she had to do. Despite her anger at him, she couldn't leave Highgate without seeing Jed one last time. She had to try to talk to him. At the very least she had to try to find out for sure what he thought she'd done, why things had gone so terribly wrong the night before.

After his treatment of her, she instinctively wanted to avoid him. He'd been so cruel; he'd made such a fool of her. Yet she had to know the truth. Despite everything, she still loved him so much that she felt as if her heart were breaking.

She checked her watch. It was only seven—much too early to go to his dorm. No one would be up. But she had to go somewhere. She felt cooped up staying in her room.

So she set out in the morning air and headed toward the stables. A ride would help her compose herself, clear her head enough so she could choose carefully the words she'd say to Jed. Only when she was halfway to the stables did she remember that Duster was gone. Jeff had taken him back to Ryan Acres the day before. With no horse to ride, Caitlin had no choice but to retrace her steps and burn off her anxiety by walking from one end of the campus to the other.

At eight-thirty she decided she could try Jed's dorm. Despite her resolve, she was nervous when she raised the brass knocker on the front door. In a moment the boys' housemaster greeted her.

"I know it's early," Caitlin said in a rush, "but I

have a very important message for Jed Michaels. Would it be too much trouble to ask you to wake him? I have to leave in a few hours—"

"But Jed's already gone."

Caitlin stared at the man. "He has?"

"Yes, last night. He came back from the dance, called a taxi, and left."

"You're sure?"

"Well, yes." The older man gave her a sympathetic look. "Yesterday afternoon he told me he was leaving and asked if he could put his luggage down in the hall by the door."

"Oh." Caitlin swallowed. "Well . . . thank you. I'm sorry to have bothered you."

"No problem. Today's going to be hectic anyway."

Caitlin turned, went down the steps, and headed back across the lawns. If she'd felt miserable and full of pain before, she felt devastated now. Jed was gone. She had no reason not to believe the housemaster. He kept a careful check on the boys in the dorm. But why did Jed leave without telling her? He'd known the previous afternoon that he was leaving that night. Why hadn't he said anything to her at the prom?

Her anguish was unbearable. Now there was no chance to talk to him, no chance to explain herself and try to work things out.

As she ran across the lawns, she was certain Jed had learned about her secret. Nothing else could have made him run off as he had; nothing else could have caused him to act so coldly toward her.

Caitlin ran back to the girls' dorm. Maybe Emily

84

knew more than she was willing to admit the night before. She had to find out. It was a long way back, but Caitlin quickly ran up the hill to the girls' dorm, pounded up the stairs to the third floor, then down the hall to Emily's room. Without knocking, she opened the door.

Emily had just rolled over on her bed, the noise from Caitlin's running footsteps having awakened her. She opened her eyes and stared hazily at the girl in the doorway.

"Caitlin, is that you?"

"Emily, I'm sorry to wake you up. Jed's gone. Did you know?"

"Jed? But my dad's not supposed to pick him up till eleven."

"I just talked to the housemaster. He said Jed had his bags packed and that he'd taken a taxi when he got home last night."

Swinging her legs over the side of the bed, Emily rubbed her eyes and shook her head to push away her sleepiness. She ran her fingers through her tousled hair. "I'd better call my parents." She stumbled to the dresser. "I need some change."

"Here." Caitlin saw a pile of coins on the dresser before Emily did and handed her the money. The two of them walked down to the end of the hall to the pay phone. Emily inserted the coins and dialed.

Caitlin waited in agony as the phone rang.

"Oh, hi, Dad," Emily said in a moment. "Yeah, it's me. How are you?" And after a short pause. "Oh, I'm great . . . great. Yeah, I know you'll be here in a couple of hours. But listen, the reason I called. Is Jed there?"

Again a moment of silence. "He did?" Caitlin studied Emily's face as the girl listened to the conversation on the other end of the phone. "Okay, Dad, okay. I'll see you in a couple of hours."

She hung up the phone and turned to Caitlin. "Jed spent the night at my parents' house. My mom just left a little while ago to take him to the airport."

"Oh, no." Caitlin leaned against the wall. She could barely keep from breaking out into sobs again.

"What happened, Caitlin?" Emily asked, confused. "I don't understand."

"Oh, Emily." Caitlin started to cry and fell into her friend's arms. "Up until last night everything was perfect . . . perfect!"

"Come back to my room. Sara's gone. We can talk there."

The two girls sat on Emily's bed. Emily tried hard to coax the words out, but Caitlin kept silent. She couldn't tell her story to Emily either. No one could know the truth.

After an hour her tears subsided and Caitlin rose. "I'd better go back to my room. Rollins will be here in a little while. Can I call you over the summer, Emily?"

"Don't be silly." Emily tried to laugh. "Of course you can. We'll keep in touch. Just because Jed's acting so strangely doesn't mean we have to!"

"I was going to ask you, have you found out what hospital Diana's in? I've been thinking about her. Maybe if we sent her some cards or some-thing . . ."

"I've been waiting to find out myself. Let me ask Laurence again. Maybe I'll see you later today. Otherwise, I'll call you next week. Are you sure you're okay?"

Caitlin nodded, biting her lip. "Yeah, yeah. I'll be fine." She tried to smile. "Thanks, Emily. I didn't mean to drop all this on you."

"Don't worry about it. What are friends for?"

Somehow Caitlin made it through the rest of the day without collapsing. If Rollins noticed her eyes were red and that she was unusually quiet and withdrawn, he made no mention of it as he and Jeff, the stable hand, moved the rest of Caitlin's belongings out of her room and into the van.

She had one very weak moment when she hugged Ginny good-bye on the front steps. "I'm going to miss you," Caitlin cried.

"Oh, I'm going to miss you, too." Ginny's voice was choked up when she spoke. "You sure you're going to be all right?"

"I'm fine now, Ginny. Really I am," Caitlin said.

"You'll write to me, okay? Listen, I want you to come visit me at home for a weekend, okay?"

"I will. Will you come to Ryan Acres?"

"Just tell me when, and I'll be there." Ginny leaned back, keeping her hands on Caitlin's shoul-ders. She looked into Caitlin's eyes. "I still don't understand what happened to you and Jed last night, but call me if you want to talk."

"I will. Gin, you're my best friend."

"Yeah," Ginny said. "We have stuck together, haven't we?"

"Miss Ryan," Rollins called from behind her, "the van's ready. Will you be following us in your car?"

"I'll be right there," Caitlin said.

She and Ginny gave each other one long hug, then Caitlin turned and hurried down the stairs. She didn't have the heart to look back.

9

Regina Ryan was waiting at the door when they arrived. When Caitlin saw her grandmother, she tried to force all the unpleasant thoughts from her mind. She pulled her car to a stop on the drive behind the van, left the keys in it so Rollins could move it later, and hurried up the front stairs.

Regina put an arm around her granddaughter's shoulders and extended her cheek for a kiss. "So, you are home at last for the summer. We'll have a quiet evening tonight. Tomorrow the Lowerys and their children are coming for brunch and tennis."

"How *are* Mr. and Mrs. Lowery?" Caitlin had to force herself to ask the questions she knew her grandmother wanted to hear.

"Fine. We're coming closer and closer to an agreement over the mines."

"I'm glad."

Her grandmother studied Caitlin's face. "Your eyes look red. Is something wrong?"

Caitlin swallowed. "No. Just an allergy, I think."

"Really? Perhaps we should have Dr. Carter look at you. When was your last physical?"

"Oh, last year. But I'm fine, Grandmother. Really."

"Humph. Well, perhaps a good night's rest will do the trick. Your prom was last night, wasn't it? How was it?"

"Very nice." Caitlin couldn't trust her voice to say any more.

"You went with Jed?"

"Yes."

"Are you still planning to visit him this summer?"

So her grandmother *hadn't* forgotten. All this time she'd left her and Jed wondering, and all this while she'd been thinking about it and probably had made a decision.

It was too late now. Caitlin wouldn't allow any emotion to show on her face as she spoke. "When you didn't give us an answer, we decided against it," she told her grandmother.

"Don't take it too hard. Jed's a sweet boy, and I'm sure you'll see him in the fall." Regina Ryan began leading Caitlin down the hallway. "I've had Margaret set a late lunch for us on the patio since it's such a beautiful day. I thought afterward we'd go over to the club and sign you up for all the summer programs . . ."

Caitlin let her grandmother talk on. She couldn't bring herself to think of summer. She couldn't think of anything at the moment.

The next morning Caitlin was out of bed early after yet another night of fitful sleep. To keep herself from thinking about Jed, she tore into her bags and boxes and unpacked the things she would need during the summer. She realized Margaret might get upset with her for doing her job, but Caitlin didn't care; she had a burning need to keep busy.

After she finished, she put on her riding clothes and went out to the barn. She had Jeff saddle up Duster, and she set out over the grounds. She gave the horse quite a workout, running him at a gallop over the riding trail that snaked through several acres of pine and birch woods. She didn't stop until they'd climbed up the trail, past the woods, to a scrub-filled clearing at the top of the hill. It was the highest point around for miles.

Caitlin got off Duster, tied his reins around a young black locust tree, and leaned against an outcropping of shale. She began to cry uncontrollably. This had been one of her favorite spots at Ryan Acres, one of the places she used to go to whenever she needed an escape. But on this warm June morning, it offered her no solace. Everywhere she looked she saw Jed. The last time she'd gone up there had been with him, to show him the incredible beauty of the spot. Her heart heavy with sadness, Caitlin wondered if she'd ever be able to stop thinking of Jed.

She couldn't remain there; the memories were too painful. So she remounted Duster and, more slowly this time, retraced her path back to the barn. Just as she finished putting Duster away, she remembered that the Lowerys were coming to visit.

Caitlin glanced at her watch, and shook her head. They had probably already arrived. Quickly she ran to the house, hoping her grandmother hadn't been trying to find her.

From the stern look she got from her grandmother, Caitlin could tell she had been missed. "Oh, there you are, dear," Mrs. Ryan said, extending her arm to her granddaughter as she entered the living room.

"Hi, Mr. and Mrs. Lowery," Caitlin said, smiling.

Mr. Lowery smiled broadly. "Caitlin, this is my daughter, Julie, and my son, Ken."

"Nice to meet you." Caitlin surveyed her guests. Julie was around her age, an attractive girl with reddish-blond hair, which she wore tied back with a scarf. She was dressed very casually in white shorts and a red- and white-striped tank top. Her brother was several years younger, a little on the pudgy side, with freckles on his face and arms.

Ordinarily Caitlin would have dreaded having to keep them company, but they were a welcome diversion that day. "Would you like to play a game of tennis?" she asked politely.

"You got a horse?" Ken asked, eyeing her outfit.

"I just took him out for a little ride," Caitlin explained.

Mrs. Ryan stepped in. "Caitlin, show Julie the courts, will you? Ken, why don't you come with us out to the pool."

"Does it have a water slide?" he asked.

Mrs. Ryan looked pained. "We have a diving board," she announced.

"All right."

Before going to the courts, Caitlin showed Julie to her room, leaving her there as she went into her bathroom and changed quickly into a tennis dress.

"Gosh, are these all your clothes?" Julie asked when she returned. She was pointing to Caitlin's open walk-in closet.

"Most of them," Caitlin answered. "Some of my winter things are in the guest bedroom across the hall."

Julie continued looking around the room. "You've got a neat stereo," she said. "I've been begging my dad to get me a new one. He says maybe for Christmas, but I'm not getting my hopes up. Of course I could buy one with the money I'll make this summer, but I'm planning on putting that in my college fund."

"You have a job? My grandmother told me you'd be coming back later this summer for a visit." As Caitlin talked she led Julie out of her room and toward the stairs.

"I'm going to be working as a counselor at a day camp. Too bad I can't make it back here. I'd love to be able to stay for a while. Tennis, horses. A pool. You're really lucky, Caitlin. Living here must be like being on a permanent vacation."

If it were only true, Caitlin thought ruefully. She'd have gladly traded all her material possessions for the one thing she lacked—love.

In the days that followed, Caitlin gave in to her

grandmother's wishes and went to the Mountain Gate Country Club to swim and play tennis and just be around other people. It occupied her time, but it didn't make her happy or rid her of her painful thoughts. Whenever she was able to get her mind off Jed for a few moments, she quickly felt overwhelmed with the guilt she continued to feel about Ian and Diana.

In fact, the first week after she got home, she received an answer to the letter she'd written to Ian at his new school. It was a short note from Mrs. Foster, telling her how happy Ian was to have heard from her. "He misses you very much," Mrs. Foster wrote. "I don't know what your plans are for the summer, but if you have the time, please drop him a line again. It helps to know you still care about him."

Caitlin wiped away her tears and began another letter to Ian right then and there. She sent it off with an old book she'd found on her bookshelf about Babar the Elephant. It was the only thing she could do to help him now.

Caitlin knew in her heart that Ian was getting the best help possible, but it didn't erase the knowledge that it was her carelessness that had put him in the wheelchair. And it didn't stop her from thinking that Jed had probably found out and now wanted to have nothing to do with her.

Caitlin had hoped that Jed would try to contact her at Ryan Acres, but day after day passed with no letter from him. Still, she wondered what he was doing. Did he round up cattle all day long?

Did he ever think of her at all? Even if he were angry with her, she couldn't believe he could have wiped away, as if they'd meant nothing, the months of togetherness they'd shared.

Caitlin agonized over it. In her beautiful room with its twin canopied beds and fireplace, she wrote a letter to him, then tore it up. She started another, then tore it up. After two more tries, she gave up. They just weren't right. She couldn't get the words to come out the way she wanted them to. She wanted to say so much, to make him truly understand what she was going through. But how could she do it?

A week after she'd gotten home, she got a call from Emily.

"I've found out where Diana is," Emily told her over the phone. "Laurence traced her. She's in a hospital in a town up near Martinsburg. Apparently there are a couple of doctors there who've done a lot of work with anorectics. And the hospital also has facilities to take care of people who've had nervous breakdowns and stuff like that."

"Nervous breakdown? You told me she had anorexia."

"Apparently she's worse off than we thought."

"Has—has Laurence heard anything about how she's doing?" The blood drained from Caitlin's face.

"No. He himself just found out where she was. But he's going to go up to visit her soon."

Caitlin's mind was working furiously. Martinsburg. That was only about forty-five minutes away. Perhaps she would get up to see Diana, too. But there was another question on her mind. "Have you heard anything from Jed?"

Emily hesitated. "No. He hasn't called, and I'm too upset to call him. I don't understand, Caitlin. What happened? Do you know why he left without saying good-bye?"

At Emily's words Caitlin felt her throat tightening. She felt as if she were going to cry all over again. "I don't know either, Emily, but if you do talk to him, tell him I love him. I've been trying to write him a letter. . . ."

"So have I. I finally mailed one yesterday. I'll let you know if he writes back."

"He *is* coming back, isn't he?" Caitlin asked worriedly.

"As far as I know."

Caitlin was depressed when she got off the phone, but already a plan was forming in her mind, and the more she thought of it, the better she felt. As she climbed into the sunken tub in her adjoining bathroom that night, she began to plan a course of action.

Two days later, after her grandmother had left for her office at Ryan Mining, Caitlin got into her car and drove to the nearest small town. She made stops at the local department store, pharmacy, and discount store. With her purchases under her arm, she walked to her car, drove back to Ryan Acres, then carried her purchases up to her room.

She went into the bathroom, wiped off all the makeup, tied back her hair severely, and fastened it in a tight bun at the back of her neck with the hair combs and pins she'd bought.

She studied herself. Yes, she already looked different, she decided, but not nearly enough. Using some of the makeup techniques she had learned in the drama club, she went to work on her face. She opened the compact of pressed powder she'd bought and spread it all over her face, even over her dark eyelashes. The coating of powder gave her a pale and anemic look, and her blue eyes seemed washed out now. Next she dabbed some blue eye shadow and dark foundation under her eyes to create deep shadows, and smoothed some more foundation into the laugh lines beside her mouth. Her face now looked drawn and terribly plain, her striking features faded. Caitlin nodded, but she wasn't quite satisfied. She smeared a pale, almost white lipstick over her otherwise red lips. She grinned to herself. No one would know her now for the glamorous Caitlin Ryan.

Caitlin went to the next bag of her purchases and pulled out a pair of narrow-rimmed glasses. The lenses were clear glass, and she could see through them easily, but they changed the character of her face even more, and completed her disguise.

Then she put on a brand-new pair of baggy jeans and a shapeless, navy-blue, short-sleeved cotton shirt. The outfit obscured her figure, and the worn-out sneakers she added were the finishing touch.

Caitlin stood before the full-length, triple-sided mirror in her dressing room and surveyed the results. She grinned. She looked as if she'd just come off a farm. Even her own grandmother wouldn't recognize her now.

Going back to the bathroom, Caitlin undid all the costuming she'd done in the past hour. She neatly folded the clothes and washed her face. She was humming to herself, ready to put her plan into action.

The next day she'd have to go to the club to play tennis in the morning; otherwise, her grandmother would get suspicious. But she'd leave before lunch. That would give her time to drive to a fast-food restaurant she knew just out of town, order lunch, then go to the ladies' room and change into her new disguise. Then it would take her at least thirty minutes more to drive to Martinsburg. Once she was there and found her way to the hospital, she would go to the employment office and ask for a place as a volunteer nurse's aide. To her knowledge, hospitals never refused volunteer workers. Somehow or other she would work her way to Diana. She'd help her in whatever way she could, without Diana ever recognizing who she was. Diana would recover, and Caitlin's conscience would be eased—completely and finally, she hoped.

Yes, she thought as she climbed into her lacy-covered bed later that evening, it was a good idea.

She'd be equal to Jed's love, even if he never knew it, and she'd be helping a person she'd wronged, inadvertent though it may have been. She snuggled her head into her pillow, and for the first time in days, Caitlin Ryan slept like a baby.

10

Caitlin was afraid her secret plan would be written all over her face the next morning, but her grandmother noticed nothing unusual as they ate a quick breakfast together.

"Marjorie Hayward tells me your tennis game is improving, Caitlin," Mrs. Ryan said as Margaret poured her another cup of tea.

"She's a good player. She makes me work hard," Caitlin said, referring to one of her regular tennis partners. Although her stomach was a jumble of nerves, she forced herself to finish the croissant on her plate. "Maybe you can watch us play sometime," she added, trying to sound as normal as possible.

Mrs. Ryan rested her bone china cup on its saucer. "Not today," she said. "I've got meetings all day long."

"Will you be home for dinner?"

"Probably not. If I am late, go ahead and eat without me." Mrs. Ryan finished off her tea, touched her lips to her linen napkin, and rose. She came around the table to place a kiss on Caitlin's cheek. "I shall see you later. Have a good day."

"I will, Grandmother. You, too."

Caitlin played three smashing sets of tennis that morning. Her new resolve showed in her game as she beat Marjorie easily: 6–1, 6–1, 6–0. Then she showered quickly and left the country club to drive north. She stopped at a fast-food restaurant, as she'd planned. She was too excited to eat but ordered a hamburger and Coke anyway, so she wouldn't arouse suspicion. After taking a few bites she went to the ladies' room with her tote bag to change into her costume.

Just to be safe, after paying her check she left the restaurant by the side door. Then, grinning to herself, she climbed into her car and headed north once more.

She had no trouble finding the town near Martinsburg where the hospital was located; by questioning the attendant at the local gas station, she got directions to the hospital.

Caitlin's anxiety grew as she parked her car and started toward the main entrance of the small hospital. What if they refused to let her volunteer? Except for Ian she really didn't have much experience working with sick people, and she didn't dare mention too many details about him.

Lifting her chin and squaring her shoulders, she pushed any doubts from her mind. She was on a mission of good, convinced that fate wouldn't allow anything to go wrong.

She found the small personnel office and went to

the receptionist's desk. A black woman in her twenties looked up.

"May I help you?"

"Yes, I'd like to apply for volunteer work."

"Can you give me your name and address?" The young woman smiled. "Then I'll let you speak to Mrs. Brand. She's in charge of our volunteer program."

"Karen Martin," Caitlin said, "R.D. One, Gaylord, Virginia." She'd chosen the town from a road sign she'd seen on the way up.

"And your telephone number?"

"I don't have one yet. It's just being installed. I've just moved." Caitlin didn't like having to tell too many lies, but this one was necessary.

The receptionist wrote down the information, then looked back up at Caitlin. "Would you wait just a minute, and I'll call Mrs. Brand."

In a few minutes, the receptionist motioned for Caitlin to follow her into the next room. "Mrs. Brand," she said, introducing her, "this is Karen Martin."

The woman smiled. "Have a seat." She indicated the chair by the side of her desk. "We're always looking for good people to help here. Of course, it's not easy work. Do you have any experience?"

"I've done some work with a paraplegic child, but I like helping people."

"That's a good reason to come to us. You're still in school?"

"Yes. I'd like to work for the summer."

"We encourage that." Mrs. Brand nodded. "Since you don't have any experience in hospitals,

I'd like to start you out with the group bringing around reading material. . . ."

Fifteen minutes later, after Mrs. Brand had explained the schedule and a bit about the hospital itself, Caitlin was on her way upstairs to pick up her uniform and begin her first day as a volunteer.

It turned out to be easier than she'd thought. The hospital wasn't that big, and by bringing around magazines and books to the patients, she was sure she'd become familiar with the entire place in no time. Although she wasn't able to find Diana by the time she had to leave, she was confident she would soon.

Caitlin arrived back at Ryan Acres just before five o'clock, well before her grandmother came home. Although her first day had been exhausting and she hadn't found Diana, she felt good. She was doing something to undo the wrong she'd done in the past.

The next few days at the hospital went smoothly. Caitlin proved herself to be a hard and diligent worker. She asked to be and was assigned to the women's floor, figuring that the most likely place to find Diana.

Yet when she finally saw Diana two days later, Caitlin almost didn't recognize her. Caitlin had entered one of the semiprivate rooms on her regular rounds with her magazine trolley and nearly jumped in shock when she read the name on the chart. Not only was the girl on the bed emaciated, but her face was ghostly pale, and her blond hair was limp and thinning. She lay unmoving on the sheets with intravenous tubes feeding into her arm.

Although Diana seemed to be in a daze, Caitlin still felt a moment's fear that she would see through her disguise. Yet she forced herself to smile. "Hi, there, how are you today?" she asked cheerfully.

Diana didn't answer. She just stared right through Caitlin as if she weren't there.

"I've brought some great magazines and books. Can I get you something?"

Diana continued to lie there unresponsively.

Caitlin felt her heart sinking to her toes. Diana was worse off than she'd imagined. All the good feelings she'd had since she'd started at the hospital were swept away by a tremendous wave of guilt. She grabbed the handle of the trolley to steady herself.

"Diana, please say something," Caitlin finally pleaded.

"She won't answer you," came a voice from the other side of the curtain in the semiprivate room.

Caitlin stepped forward and looked around at the elderly woman in the bed on the other side. "Did you say something?"

"No use talking to her. It's a sad thing, but since I've been here—over a week now—I haven't heard her say a word. She just lays there like that—staring off at nothing or sleeping."

"Aren't they doing anything to help her?"

"Well, sure they are. A couple of doctors come in here every day and sit there an hour or so with her, talking to her. It don't do no good. Don't know what it is she's got."

Caitlin swallowed. It seemed strange to be talking about Diana's condition as if she weren't in the room, but from the blank look on her face, it was obvious that nothing the older woman had said had registered.

"You can give me some of those magazines." The woman's voice cut into Caitlin's thoughts.

"Sure." Again she forced herself to smile. "Which ones would you like?"

"Oh, that *Woman's Day*, and I guess the *Family Circle*. My daughter's going to bring up my crocheting, and I want to see if they've got any new patterns."

"Will you be in the hospital long?" Caitlin tried to feign interest in the older woman, but her mind was on Diana.

"Oh, just a few more days from what the doc says."

"I'm glad to hear that." Caitlin handed the woman the magazines and started to leave. "I'll be back tomorrow."

"See you then, dear."

As soon as Caitlin had a few free minutes, she went to the nurses' station on the floor. She had to know more about Diana's condition. She had to find a way of working with her.

What the head nurse, Eileen Crenshaw, told her wasn't encouraging. "The trauma that brought on the anorexia has made her turn inside herself. It's as if she's created her own world and totally shut out the real world. The best psychiatrist on the staff

105

is working with her, but you know, these cases are really hard. The causes can go so deep."

Caitlin cringed. "She looks like she's just fading away."

"Unfortunately, in a way she is. It seems she caused an accident that crippled a little boy. Apparently she felt so guilty about it, she starved herself for months. It was really touch and go when she was first brought in."

"I'd like to help. Do you think I can work with her?"

Ms. Crenshaw gave her a skeptical look. "What can you do? If Dr. Pierce hasn't been able—"

"Can't I at least try?" Caitlin pleaded. "Maybe it would help if someone her own age was talking to her. I can relate to what she's going through."

"You can?"

"I—I had a friend who was anorectic," Caitlin said quickly. "Look, I could put in an hour a day with her. I don't see how it could hurt."

The nurse seemed to brighten. "Well, it's not really up to me. But I can check with her doctor."

"Great. I can start tomorrow."

"I'll talk to Dr. Pierce in the morning."

"Thanks! Thanks so much."

Caitlin showed up promptly at the nurses' station after her rounds the next day. She'd finished her duties with an hour to spare—the hour she planned to give to Diana.

Eileen Crenshaw smiled when she saw her. "The doctor said okay. He doesn't know if it will do any good, but he's sure it can't hurt either. Do let us know if you see any change."

Caitlin nodded. "I'll keep a daily record. Thanks again."

She hurried to Diana's room and quietly drew up a chair beside her bed. Diana seemed to be staring at some point halfway up the opposite wall. Her eyes were dull and lifeless. Caitlin had to force herself not to cry.

Thinking that Diana might respond to touch, Caitlin took the hand that wasn't connected to the intravenous tubes and held it gently in her own. Diana's skin felt warm, but despite the gentle pressure of Caitlin's fingers, the ailing girl's hand remained limp. Caitlin then spoke softly, directing her voice toward Diana's ear.

"I'm a friend, Diana. I want to help you very much. I want to see you get better—and you *can* if you'll only try. I know it's going to take time, but I'm going to come visit you every day that I can. Even if you won't talk to me, I'll keep talking to you. I want you to know that someone cares very much that you get better."

For the rest of the hour, Caitlin interspersed words of encouragement with gentle actions. She smoothed Diana's tangled hair; she straightened the sheets. She didn't dare move Diana or lift her head from the pillow, but she did what she could to try to make her more comfortable.

The hour went too quickly, and nothing she'd done had evoked the slightest response from Diana. Truly she was fading away; it was as if she'd lost all her will to live.

Caitlin was close to tears when she finally dragged herself from the room. Her first day working with Diana had brought no results. But she wasn't going to give up. She was determined to make Diana well. She *had* to!

11

For three agonizing weeks Caitlin sat with Diana, trying to get some reaction from her. Day after day she read to the unresponsive girl, held her hand, talked to her, and brought her fresh flowers. But Diana either stared vacantly into space or slept without stirring. Nothing worked. Every afternoon Caitlin left the hospital depressed and exhausted.

Caitlin had always been used to getting what she wanted—and doing whatever she had to do to get it. Now, she seemed to be up against a problem that she couldn't overcome. She spent hours in her room, thinking about what she could do. One Saturday she went to the library and took out several books on anorexia nervosa and on mental disorders. She was careful to keep them hidden in her walk-in closet during the day; she didn't want either of the maids to find them and say something to her grandmother. At night Caitlin pored over them, trying to find some clue that would help her bring Diana back to reality. She could find nothing. But she was determined not to give up.

Finally, on the verge of desperation, Caitlin came

up with a plan that might—just might—work. But Caitlin knew that following it through was going to be the hardest thing she'd ever done.

The elderly woman had been discharged, so Caitlin and Diana were alone in the room. The day Caitlin put the plan into effect, she held Diana's hand and took a deep breath. Then she leaned close to Diana's ear. Her voice held a plea. "Diana, please listen to me. You weren't responsible for Ian Foster's poisoning. It wasn't your fault at all. You didn't leave the shed door unlocked. Can you hear me, Diana? You don't have to blame yourself. You don't have to be sick because of it. Someone else left the shed unlocked. It was her fault, not yours. And Ian's getting better." She reached up and stroked Diana's cheek softly. "Please listen, Diana. Please hear me. I want you to get better. You don't have to punish yourself anymore!"

Caitlin sat back in her chair, pushed her glasses back up on her nose, and wiped her brow with her free hand. It had taken so much out of her to make that admission aloud. She prayed that it would do some good.

Diana didn't move. Caitlin sighed deeply. Telling Diana the truth had to work, it had to! Leaning forward and touching Diana's hand, Caitlin started again, her voice stronger. "Diana, listen to me— listen!" Again she told Diana that it wasn't her fault, that she wasn't responsible. "And Ian is getting better, Diana. He's getting better." Her words were forceful now.

Still holding Diana's hand, Caitlin leaned back, exhausted, in the chair and closed her eyes.

Suddenly she thought she felt Diana's hand move, ever so slightly. Instantly alert, Caitlin opened her eyes and sat up, rigid, staring at Diana.

Suddenly Diana shuddered. "Ian." Her voice was little more than a hoarse whisper.

Caitlin nearly jumped from her chair. Moving close to the bed again, she squeezed Diana's hand tighter. "It's all right, Diana. It wasn't your fault. You understand me, don't you? You *weren't* responsible."

"Not—my—fault?" the girl asked weakly.

"No, it wasn't. It wasn't your fault at all! It was m—" Caitlin stopped herself, unable to make a full confession. "Someone else left the shed unlocked. You have to get better, Diana. We all love you—we want you to get well."

Without releasing Diana's hand, Caitlin reached up with her other hand to press the nurse's call button.

The effort of talking was too much of a strain, and Diana closed her eyes.

The next moment a nurse came hurrying into the room.

"Is something wrong?" The nurse was worried.

"No—it's wonderful. She's talking again!" Caitlin was so happy, she felt as if she were going to cry.

The nurse's eyes widened in shock.

"I know you're tired, Diana," Caitlin urged, "but can you just open your eyes a minute?"

In a second Diana's lids lifted slowly.

"I don't believe it. It's a miracle," the nurse said.

"You can hear me, can't you?" Caitlin asked.

"Yes," Diana whispered.

"I'll get the doctor and Ms. Crenshaw," the young woman said quickly. "Stay with her until we get back, will you?"

For an instant there was a confused look on Diana's face, then she closed her eyes again. Yet this time when Caitlin squeezed her hand, she returned the pressure lightly.

Over the next few days, Diana improved slowly but steadily. She was still hazy and unable—or unwilling—to remember much of what had gone on in her life before she'd entered the hospital, but her will to live apparently had returned. She wanted to recover now, and to Caitlin's relief, Diana still showed no signs of recognizing her.

With the hospital's approval, Caitlin spent all her time with Diana, coaxing her along. Neither Dr. Pierce, Diana's doctor, nor Mrs. Brand had any objection. They agreed that Caitlin's time was better spent working her miracle with the girl no one had thought would recover.

Although she was still being fed intravenously, Dr. Pierce now had Diana on a light diet as well. One afternoon, as Caitlin was sitting with Diana, Dr. Pierce came into the room.

"After nearly starving herself like she has," he explained to Caitlin, "we have to go slowly with the food. Gaining weight too quickly would be as much of a shock to her system as was the sudden weight loss." He wrinkled his brow. "I'd still like to know exactly what it was you did, how you got her to respond. Dr. Morgan and I have been working with her for weeks with no results."

"I just talked to her and held her hand," Caitlin explained, as she had when he had asked her that first afternoon. "Ms. Crenshaw told me that there'd been some kind of an accident that might have led to her making herself sick. I just told her that it wasn't her fault, that we all cared about her and wanted to see her get better."

"Well, Miss Martin, you seem to have done the trick. Keep up the good work."

And Caitlin did work hard. As tired as she was, the progress she was making with Diana kept her spirits up. She couldn't wait to get to the hospital each day, though keeping her trips a secret from her grandmother was difficult.

Caitlin had developed a routine of going to the country club every morning to play tennis with Marjorie, a socially active woman who was one of the few at the club able to beat Caitlin at the game she played so well. Marjorie always ran off to play golf in the afternoons, so she never noticed Caitlin's departure for the hospital.

Soon after she started working there, Caitlin had written to Ginny. She felt she couldn't risk having anyone, even her good friend, find out about her secret activities, so she had told Ginny that her grandmother had planned so many activities that summer that she didn't see how she would be able to get together with her. Fortunately for Caitlin her grandmother's social calendar really wasn't so busy. Mrs. Ryan had become so involved with the union negotiations that she hadn't had time to go to the club herself or even entertain other guests at Ryan Acres.

But Caitlin's luck wasn't destined to last for long.

"I'm taking the morning off," her grandmother said to her over the breakfast table the next Tuesday morning. "We haven't had much time to spend together so far this summer. I thought we might go riding."

Caitlin thought wistfully about Duster, whom she'd nearly had to abandon to keep up her hectic schedule.

"I'm sorry, Grandmother, but I've made plans to play tennis," Caitlin said quickly. Of course, she couldn't add that she would be leaving the club directly for the hospital.

"On second thought," Mrs. Ryan continued, "why don't I join you? I haven't had a good game of tennis in an age. I can play a few sets, then have lunch, and then I'll go on to the office."

Caitlin nearly choked on her orange juice. "But I'm supposed to play with Marjorie."

"I'm sure she wouldn't mind standing out so that we could play."

Caitlin tried to think up another excuse. She couldn't very well leave for the hospital with her grandmother watching her. But it seemed to be out of her hands. "No, I guess she wouldn't mind," she said finally.

"Excellent," Regina smiled, pleased with her decision. "We'll need two cars. What time did you reserve the court for?"

"Ten."

"Good. I'll go change into my tennis clothes."

All the way to the club, Caitlin fumed. Darn her grandmother, messing up her plans again! She was never there when Caitlin needed her, but always managed to interfere when she was least wanted. If she intended to play several sets and then have lunch, too, that meant Caitlin would be two hours late to the hospital!

Well, Caitlin decided, she would make sure those sets were over as quickly as possible, and then find some excuse to get out of lunch.

When they arrived at the courts, they had a half-hour wait. The tennis pro apologized profusely, explaining that the early-bird tournament had run over. As the minutes ticked by, Caitlin grew more and more irritated, and when their court was finally free, she vented her anger in her game.

Her serves were like pistol shots, unsettling her grandmother, who was used to a more leisurely game. Caitlin didn't care. She slammed her returns across the net, playing with every bit of skill she possessed.

At the end of the first set, which Caitlin won 6–0, her grandmother's cheeks looked flushed. It was a hot morning, and Caitlin was feeling the heat herself. She hoped her grandmother would decide to call it quits, but Regina Ryan was made of sterner stuff. They went on to the second set, and again Caitlin showed no mercy. Her irritation increased the longer they played. She had to get to the hospital!

She won the second set easily. Regina Ryan went

to the side of the court for a towel. Caitlin waited for the older woman to say that she'd had enough, but Mrs. Ryan only wiped her brow. "Your game has improved remarkably," she called out over the net. Even though she sounded winded, she returned to the court. "Shall we?"

Caitlin served once again, and Regina Ryan valiantly returned the ball. The older woman was tiring and feeling the heat, but Caitlin played with all the intensity she'd shown in the first set, winning the last set 6–1.

"Well," her grandmother said a little tersely as they walked to the locker room, "playing with Marjorie seems to have done your game a world of good." Mrs. Ryan looked exhausted, although Caitlin knew her grandmother would never admit how tired she was.

It was twelve-thirty by the time they'd showered and dressed, and as they left the women's locker room, Mrs. Ryan checked her watch.

"It you don't mind," she said, trying to hide her fatigue, "I think I'll skip lunch and go straight to the office. I shall see you tonight."

"Yes, Grandmother." Caitlin's tone was meek, but as her grandmother walked away, she smiled to herself in satisfaction.

A few moments after Regina Ryan drove off in her silver Mercedes-Benz, Caitlin sped to her car. When she stopped at a gas station on her way to the hospital to change, she didn't have time to take her usual pains with her disguise. She powdered her face and drew back her hair into its severe bun, but only lightly rubbing in the shadow under her eyes, forgetting her glasses completely. Within minutes she was back in the car again, but even taking all the shortcuts she knew, she arrived at the hospital over an hour late.

On her way to Diana's room, she stopped at the nurses' station to explain why she was delayed.

"Oh, Karen." The nurse on duty looked up. "I'm glad you're here. There's someone who'd like to meet you."

"But I've still got to change into my uniform and see Diana. I'm late."

The nurse smiled. "Don't worry. She's all right. She had visitors today and is resting now. Just wait a second." She turned and stepped over to one of the small offices behind the station and spoke to someone inside. In a moment she returned, a white-coated man walking beside her. "Karen, this is Dr. Westlake, director of the hospital. Dr. Westlake, Karen Martin."

Dr. Westlake came forward with his hand extended. He was a handsome man, tall and dark with a touch of gray at his temples. His eyes were a beautiful, clear blue. "Well, hello there." He smiled broadly. "I've been hearing a lot about you."

"You have?" Caitlin took his hand, then remembered her manners. "I mean, how do you do?"

Dr. Westlake chuckled. "You've really been working wonders with one of our patients. Dr. Pierce has been telling me about the breakthrough in Diana Chasen's condition. He says you're the one responsible."

Caitlin blushed. The hospital director congratulating *her*? "Oh, I don't know if I'm the one responsible. I just wanted to help. I didn't want to see her keep fading away."

"I've been curious." The doctor leaned his elbow on the nurses' stand and studied Caitlin. "What's your background? Have you had experience with someone who had anorexia before?"

"No—I mean, yes," she said, quickly remembering the story she had told Ms. Crenshaw. "That is, I knew someone who was anorectic. I wanted to volunteer at the hospital for the summer, and when I saw Diana, I guess I thought that maybe it could happen to me. She's about my age."

Caitlin couldn't help noticing that Dr. Westlake had never taken his eyes from her face. He looked almost puzzled. She wondered if she'd done something to upset him.

"So you're about sixteen then?"

Caitlin nodded.

"Are you from this area?"

"I just moved here."

"From another part of Virginia?"

"No, from Maryland." Caitlin repeated the story she'd fabricated on her first day there. Dr. Westlake was still studying her face, making her even more nervous. "Is—is something wrong?"

He shook his head quickly. "No, no, and I apologize for staring. You just remind me of someone."

"Oh." Caitlin relaxed. She was sure she'd never met Dr. Westlake before.

"Are you planning to go into medicine?" the doctor added.

"No, I hadn't thought of it."

"I just wondered. Sometimes volunteers your age are trying to get a taste of hospital life before entering a career in the field. He smiled again and straightened. "Well, I'm glad I had a chance to meet you. You're a welcome addition to our volunteer staff."

"Thank you very much, and it's been nice meeting you, too."

"I'm sure I'll see you again." Dr. Westlake lifted his hand in parting, and Caitlin turned and continued down the hall toward the room where volunteers changed into their uniforms. She didn't notice Dr. Westlake watching her intently.

She felt as though she were walking on air. To have the director of the hospital single her out was quite a compliment.

She quickly changed, then tucked a stray hair back into her bun. Suddenly she realized she wasn't wearing her glasses. Quickly she dug them out of her shoulder bag and put them on. After putting her bag into the locker she had been assigned, Caitlin hurried down the hall to Diana's room.

Diana was sitting up in bed with pillows propped behind her back. She was still weak and very, very thin, but her color was much better. She smiled when she saw Caitlin.

"Hi, how are you today?" Caitlin smiled. "You're looking good!"

"I had something to eat. I can't believe it—I'm actually hungry."

119

"I brought some books and magazines for you," Caitlin said as she slid the pile in her arms onto the nightstand. "We have to keep you from getting bored."

"Well, I haven't been bored today. My parents came to visit again this morning." Diana's eyes grew momentarily sad. "Daddy was so happy to see me sitting up and talking, I thought he was going to cry. When I think what I've put them through—"

"Don't think about it. You were sick. You couldn't help it."

"I know, but they were so worried. They're so grateful for what you've done for me. They'd like to meet you."

"They would?" Caitlin kept her face expressionless despite the sudden quiver in her stomach. She wasn't ready to meet Diana's parents.

"Of course! I've told them all about you and how much you've helped me, *Karen*."

There was something strange about the way Diana had emphasized Caitlin's assumed name, it made Caitlin uncomfortable. "Anybody would have done the same," she said quickly.

"Not anybody."

The conversation was edging too close to the truth. Caitlin tried to distract Diana. "Would you like me to brush your hair?" she asked.

"If you don't mind. I know it's a mess, but my arms get tired if I try to lift them."

Caitlin got the brush out of the nightstand drawer, adjusted the pillows behind Diana's back, and began gently to work out the tangles in Diana's still thin and lifeless-looking hair.

"You know, Karen," Diana said thoughtfully in a moment, "I keep thinking that I've met you before—oh, I know I haven't—but you remind me of someone."

Caitlin swallowed. First Dr. Westlake, and now Diana. "Oh, really?"

"Yes. It's your voice. You sound almost exactly like a girl I used to know at school."

Caitlin wanted to hide. She thought she'd been so careful. But how could she have been stupid enough not to think Diana would recognize her voice? "People sometimes sound alike," she said quickly.

"Mmmm. This girl was beautiful. I used to wonder what it was like to be so popular. I was always a little nervous when I was around her."

Caitlin didn't notice the sideways glance Diana was giving her. "Were you?" she said. How strange it was to hear herself talked about as if she weren't there. She was startled, too. Diana was beginning to remember things, things from the past that up until now she'd blocked out.

Diana chuckled. "I really didn't fit in at that school. Did I tell you that I went to Highgate?"

"No." Caitlin took a slow breath. "Is that a good school? I just moved to this area so I don't know much about the schools here yet."

"Highgate is this very exclusive private boarding school. All the kids there had loads of money! I was on scholarship. I never felt comfortable until I met a boy. He was so nice. I couldn't believe he

121

actually cared about me. Sometimes I wonder how's he doing now. I should have written to him, but after what happened to Ian, I just wanted to forget everything about Highgate. I felt so terrible."

The old guilt gripped Caitlin again. "It wasn't your fault," she said automatically.

Diana was silent for a moment, then asked innocently, "I've been wondering today. How did you know about the accident?"

Caitlin's hand froze in midair. She hadn't expected Diana to have remembered *anything* of what she'd told her that day to snap her out of her lethargy. "Uh, well, the nurses told me about your background."

"How did they know?"

"Your parents."

Diana didn't pursue it any further, though she remained thoughtful.

"There!" Caitlin interrupted brightly, her heart pounding so loudly she was afraid Diana would notice. "That looks much better. Let me get you a mirror so you can see."

"I don't know if I want to look at myself," Diana said.

"How about if I pull it up with a couple of barrettes? That would keep it neater."

"Sure. Anything would be an improvement."

Caitlin sighed silently. Diana was diverted for the time being—she hoped.

"You haven't told me much about yourself either, Karen. Out of all the people in the hospital, why did you pick me to help?"

"I wanted you to get better—I was sure you could. And we're the same age. It could have been me."

"Yeah. But you're giving up all the fun things you could be doing this summer."

"Oh, I have fun here."

"Haven't your parents planned any trips, or anything?"

"I don't have any parents."

Diana turned to stare at her. "You don't?"

"They died a long time ago." Caitlin didn't realize that the true pain of that statement showed clearly on her face. She was only thinking of the details she'd concocted about Karen's life. She'd kept it somewhat close to the truth, so she wouldn't contradict herself.

"I'm really sorry."

"Oh, it's all right. It happened a long time ago. I'm used to it."

"Is that why you like to work at the hospital?" Diana asked. "So you can be close to people?"

"I guess." Caitlin found Diana's questions disturbing. Maybe she should have manufactured a set of parents along with her phony address. Thinking about a mother, who'd died giving birth to her, and a father who'd abandoned her shortly after that, made Caitlin's throat tighten and ache. Caitlin had never seen her father and never wanted to. She hoped he was dead, for if she ever came across him she wouldn't hesitate to show him how much she hated him for abandoning her.

"Where are you from?" Diana held her head still

so Caitlin could fasten the barrettes, but she looked at Caitlin out of the corner of her eye.

"From Maryland."

"And you said you just moved to Virginia?"

"Right."

"Where are you staying?"

"With some relatives."

"You'll have to take up riding. Everyone around here does. Or do you ride already?"

"Well, of course! Uh—I mean," Caitlin stumbled, "I've tried it a few times." She could have kicked herself. It was unlikely that Karen Martin would be an experienced rider with the humble beginnings she'd painted for her. She had to change the subject quickly. "There!" she exclaimed. "Finished." She handed Diana a mirror. "Take a look."

Diana studied her reflection and wrinkled her nose. "Oh, the hair looks great. But I'm just so pale."

"Keep eating and resting and doing what the doctor says, and that'll go away pretty quickly," Caitlin said encouragingly.

For the rest of the afternoon, until four, when Caitlin had to leave, the girls looked through fashion magazines. Caitlin kept the conversation light and talked only about the future—never the past. She encouraged Diana to talk about the career hopes she'd almost given up. And Caitlin made up a story about how she hoped to use the experience she was getting that summer in her future medical career. It sounded to her like something Karen Martin would say.

When Caitlin left to go home, Diana was smiling

and content and seemed to be looking forward to the light dinner that would soon be delivered to the room. "See you tomorrow," she called to Caitlin.

"See you tomorrow," Caitlin said and waved.

Once Caitlin was gone, Diana leaned back against her pillows and frowned thoughtfully. Ever since she'd been strong enough to take a little interest in things, something had been gnawing away at her—Karen Martin's resemblance to a girl she'd known at Highgate. Each time Karen had been in the room, Diana had kept a close watch on her, and the more she'd studied her, the more confused she'd become. If Karen's hair hadn't been pulled back so tightly, if there'd been some color in her face, if she hadn't been wearing glasses, she would have been a double for Caitlin Ryan. In fact that day Diana had noticed the resemblance more than ever. Karen had even sounded like Caitlin.

Yet why would Caitlin Ryan be in the hospital helping her, a girl she'd barely been friendly with? Why would Caitlin pretend she was someone else? Caitlin wasn't the kind to give up so much of herself to volunteer in a hospital—especially disguised as someone as plain and unassuming as Karen Martin. The Caitlin she knew was beautiful and rich and popular and had always seemed to have everything she wanted.

Diana shook her head. Up until that afternoon, those questions had kept her doubting. It had to be a coincidence, she'd kept telling herself—people *did* look alike.

Needing to have an answer, she'd deliberately

tested Karen during their conversation, and after watching her nervous reactions to her questions and hearing some of her slips, Diana was virtually positive that Karen Martin was actually Caitlin Ryan.

But it made no sense! It made absolutely no sense!

Had something happened at school after Diana left? She'd deliberately cut off all contact with her old friends, so she had no idea what had gone on. Even though Caitlin was putting on a cheerful front, Diana could sense that, underneath it all, she was terribly unhappy about something.

What was she to do? Should she tell Caitlin she had recognized her? Should she come right out and ask her why she was there?

Diana sighed heavily and closed her eyes. She was still tired and weak—much too tired to make any decisions. She needed time to think and to pull all the pieces together. In the meantime she'd keep watching Caitlin. Diana was now convinced that sooner or later Caitlin would give some hint of her reasons herself.

12

Dr. Gordon Westlake was distracted as he entered his office at the end of the day and accepted a sheaf of messages from his secretary.

"Thanks, Miss Parks. Anything urgent?"

"Not really. Mrs. Jennings wanted you to call her tonight about a benefit dinner party tomorrow. The others are just the usual."

"Why don't you go on home, then."

"But I've left some letters for you to sign."

"None of them are that important. They can go out in the morning."

"Are you all right, Doctor?"

"Hmmmm?"

"You seem tired."

"Oh, no, just a lot on my mind—a busy day."

"Okay, good night, then."

"Good night." Dr. Westlake stepped into his private office and closed the door behind him. Sitting down behind his desk, he started glancing through the messages in his hand, then put them down on his blotter. He couldn't concentrate. He flipped open the folder of neatly typed letters lying on the side of the gleaming desk top, but at the moment he wasn't interested in reading them either.

All afternoon long, he hadn't been able to get Karen Martin out of his thoughts. It was incredible how much she reminded him of a woman he'd known long ago, a woman whom he'd tried unsuccessfully to put from his mind through all these years. The features were so similar: the perfect bone structure, the shape of the eyes, and the well-formed mouth with the bottom lip a little fuller than the top and the corners slightly turned up.

He rose from his desk and went restlessly to the window. He was being ridiculous, and he knew it. Karen Martin was no more than a young girl. The woman he was thinking of would have been nearly forty now, and he hadn't seen her in over seventeen years—not since her wealthy and power-happy mother had driven a wedge between them and taken her out of his life.

He hadn't been a doctor then, only a bone-tired, poor medical student, son of a lower middle-class mountain family. His outstanding grades had earned him a scholarship to the University of Virginia, where he met her, his Laura. They had fallen in love quickly and made plans to be married before he started his internship. Neither of them could—or wanted to—wait any longer.

Then her mother stepped in. After she'd asked about Gordon's background and he'd told her he was raised in the mountains, she'd become cool and haughty. She'd done her best to ignore him and had treated him as if he were dirt. Of course, she only behaved that way when Laura couldn't see.

But that didn't make Gordon stop loving Laura. When her mother saw this, she took more direct measures. He'd never discovered for sure what lies she'd embedded in Laura's mind. In a way that really didn't matter; what counted was that she believed them. A few days before graduation she'd left him a note, telling him that she felt deceived and disgusted by his actions. She never wanted to see him again.

When he'd tried to call her at school, he'd been told she had left. He'd tried to call her at home, but was told impersonally that she and her mother were away and would be indefinitely. He'd tried again many times after that, but he was always told the same: Mother and daughter were away.

Finally, after months and months, he gave up and put his mind back to his studies. He'd had to. Laura was lost to him, and he knew it. He had to get on with his life.

But he'd never loved anyone as he'd loved Laura—not even to this day.

He ran his fingers through his thick black hair. He realized he was being foolish. What could this young girl have to do with Laura? Yet something nagged at him, something he couldn't shake. And it was strong enough to propel him into action. He knew he had to find out more about Karen Martin.

13

Caitlin heard from Emily the following night. "I'm taking the night off from studying and thought I'd give you a call," she said. "How's your summer going, Caitlin?"

She paused. It felt strange talking to her old friend, after having spent the afternoon pretending to be someone else. "Oh, fine," she said, trying to keep her voice light. "Though nothing special, really. Lots of tennis at the club, stuff like that. So summer school agrees with you?"

"Yes. It's challenging, but there's time to have fun, too. Terry and I see each other often, which is great. But I didn't call to tell you about my life. I've got good news for you."

Caitlin's heart jumped. Had Emily heard from Jed? "Oh, what's that?" she asked, her hopes rising.

"I heard from Laurence today. He told me Diana's getting better. It looks like she's going to be all right now."

Caitlin was glad Emily couldn't see the disappointment she was feeling. "That's wonderful," she said.

"Poor Diana," Emily went on. "Turns out she was really in bad shape. But some girl at the hospital she's at took a special interest in her and saved her life. Laurence is going up to visit her tomorrow."

Caitlin had to try hard to pretend this was all news to her. "Diana's a lucky girl."

"I'll say," Emily agreed. "So have you heard from anyone else at Highgate?"

"Just from Ginny," Caitlin said, glancing at the latest letter from her roommate on her desktop. "She's up to her ears in horse shows, as you might well imagine. And I've been writing to Ian."

"How is he?"

"The same, I'm afraid. But he likes his school. His mother sent me one of his drawings."

"So he's a budding artist? Great," Emily said. "So have you heard from anyone else?"

In a voice almost as low as a whisper she added, "I got a letter from Jed."

As much as she wanted to, Caitlin couldn't contain her excitement. "You did? When?"

"Last week."

"Why didn't you tell me sooner?"

Emily paused. "I know how upset you are about what's happened."

"Emily, you've got to tell me what he said."

"He didn't say much. He's just hanging out at the ranch, not doing too much. It's what he *didn't* say that bothers me. He sounded terribly lonely.

He said living in Virginia for a year made him realize how wide open and empty Montana is."

"Did he say anything about me?"

"No," Emily admitted. "That's why I didn't tell you. He didn't mention you at all."

Caitlin didn't let Emily know how much the news depressed her. But after she got off the phone, she realized that subconsciously she had been clinging to the hope that time and distance would make him miss her and have second thoughts about the way he had treated her.

That night she tried once again to write to him, but she couldn't get the words down right.

No, she realized, after she threw the notepaper on the floor in frustration, mere words wouldn't be enough for Jed. She had to continue her masquerade and ensure that Diana got better. Only then, when she had proved herself, would she be able to approach him and make him understand.

When Caitlin walked into Diana's room the following day, her smile was as bright and cheerful as ever. But as Caitlin suspected, Diana wasn't alone. Laurence Baxter was sitting in the chair next to her bed.

Caitlin almost started to call out, "Hi, Laurence," to the tall, good-looking boy, but she caught herself just in time. Instead she turned to Diana. "How are you today?"

"Getting better all the time." Diana smiled. "Karen, I'd like you to meet an old friend of mine.

aurence Baxter, Karen Martin. Karen's the girl I've
een telling you about, Laurence."

"Nice to meet you, Karen." Laurence's voice was
riendly, but Caitlin noticed he seemed to be
xamining her. Was he able to see through her
lisguise?

"Nice to meet you, too, Laurence. You didn't tell
ne you had a boyfriend, Diana."

Diana blushed. "Laurence is like a brother to me.
He's one of the good friends I almost let slip away."

"Diana's looking good, isn't she?" Caitlin asked.

"She sure is." He reached over and squeezed
Diana's hand. "She had me worried for a while."

"She had a lot of people worried here at the
hospital," Caitlin said.

"It was great of you to work with Diana like
you've been doing."

Caitlin shrugged modestly. "You two probably
want to talk," she added. She couldn't stay in the
room with Laurence there. "I'll come back later."

"You can stay," Diana protested.

"No, I have some other things to do on the floor.
You guys have a good time. I'll see you later."

As she started to turn to leave the room, again
she noticed Laurence giving her a funny look.
Without looking back, she hurried out to the hall.

"I really feel sorry for her, Laurence." Diana
looked over at her friend after Caitlin had left. "I
think she's really unhappy. Not that she ever
complains. Unless you ask her, she never talks
about anything except my getting better."

"When you told me that Caitlin was working here, I thought you were crazy. But now I think you're right."

Diana shook her head. "When I first started feeling better, I thought Karen's voice seemed familiar. But I said to myself, 'What would Caitlin be doing here? She's gorgeous and rich. She's got everything.'" Diana frowned. "Why in the world would she disguise herself and help me? She never liked me that much."

Laurence shrugged. "I don't know her well enough to answer that. But you know that right after you left, she started going with Jed."

"Yeah, you told me." For a moment Diana's eyes grew sad, then she shook her head. "I was thinking about Jed the other day. You know, I was the one who ended our relationship. He tried to get in touch with me after I left."

"Jed's a nice guy. He wouldn't have let what happened change his feelings about you."

"I know. But even if it hadn't been for Ian's accident, it wouldn't have worked for Jed and me. We were too different. And after the accident, I just felt so terrible, so guilty. I thought if I ran away . . ."

"Your friends would have been there for you. I know Emily tried hard to get in touch with you, too. You should have at least written us."

"My mother didn't want me to have anything to do with the kids at Highgate."

"I just thought of something," Laurence mused. "Right before the end of school, I heard that Caitlin was spending a lot of time with Ian Foster."

Diana stared at him in surprise. "Are you sure?"

"Positive."

Diana suddenly thought back to something Karen—Caitlin—had said right in the beginning. "She said it wasn't my fault," she whispered suddenly. "She said someone else left the shed unlocked!"

"What are you talking about?"

"Caitlin . . . when I was so sick—when I didn't care if I lived or not—she talked to me. I don't remember a lot of what she said. Nothing mattered to me, and I was so weak. But one day I heard this voice repeating to me that it wasn't my fault . . . that I hadn't left the shed unlocked . . . that I could stop blaming myself . . . that Ian was going to be all right.

"That's when something happened inside me. I wanted to hear what this person was saying. I wanted to be alive again. But I was so sick that I thought afterward that I'd dreamed the whole thing. Maybe she just said that to get through to me."

"Why don't we just ask her?"

"No! No, don't." Diana placed her hand on his arm and looked at him in panic. "She must have a good reason for being here and pretending she's someone else. She's done so much for me, Laurence. She saved my life. Let's give her a chance. She's really unhappy, and if I give her time, I think she'll come to me and tell me why she did it."

"She might." But Laurence didn't sound convinced.

135

* * *

Diana was making great strides in her recovery. The intravenous tubes had been removed, and she'd begun to eat more substantial meals and gain weight. She had been allowed out of bed, too, and Caitlin and she practiced short walks every afternoon. At first, Diana had been sure that her legs would collapse under her, but Caitlin had kept encouraging her a few steps at a time. Now Diana was strong enough to walk up and down the hall.

Diana hadn't said a word to Caitlin about her knowledge of her true identity, but at night when the hospital was quiet, she'd tried to figure out Caitlin's reasons for disguising herself. The more she'd thought about it, the more confused she'd become. Finally one day, as they were taking their daily walk, Caitlin said something that gave Diana a clue to what might be causing some of her unhappiness.

Diana had been talking about what she should do to start making a new life for herself.

"One thing I'll do is get in touch with my old friends. I know they were all hurt when I cut them off like I did—especially the boy I was going with."

"Oh, yes . . . Jed," Caitlin said.

Diana turned to stare at her new friend's face. Caitlin was looking down, and Diana knew she'd spoken without thinking. Diana was sure she'd never mentioned Jed's name to her.

"I'm not sure where to get in touch with him," Diana continued, watching Caitlin's face, "but I'm going to write to him at his father's ranch."

Caitlin's eyes had closed momentarily behind her glasses; her face was paler than ever.

Diana was stunned at her reaction. Laurence had told her that Caitlin and Jed were going together. Why would the mention of Jed's name make Caitlin look so hurt? Had something happened between them? she wondered.

Diana quickly changed the subject, but after Caitlin had left that day, Diana picked up a pad of paper and a pen and started to write. She still had the address of Jed's father's ranch. The previous fall, when things were still good between them, he'd given it to her. She began to write:

Dear Jed,

This letter's going to come as a surprise, I know, after all the months I've ignored all my old friends. That was stupid, and from now on I'm not going to be so silly.

So much has happened since the last time I saw you that I won't even try to put it all in this letter. I'm in a hospital in Virginia now, getting better after being very, very sick. Nobody thought I was going to make it. But one girl, a volunteer at the hospital, made me realize that I had something to live for. She worked with me, sat with me, talked to me—made me try to get better. She wouldn't give up. It sounds melodramatic, but I owe her my life.

The girl I'm talking about is Caitlin Ryan, but she doesn't know I know that. She calls herself Karen Martin, and she's got herself fixed up to look so plain that unless you really studied her, you'd never recognize her.

I don't know why she's doing this, but I know there's something that's making her really unhappy. I mentioned your name the other day, and she looked as if she were going to cry. Laurence told me that you and Caitlin were going together all spring. That's one of the reasons I'm writing to you now—to see if you know what's wrong and know why she's pretending to be someone she isn't.

She's done so much for me, Jed, that I want to help her, too. Please write to me as soon as you can. I'm not going to tell her I know who she is until I hear from you.

I hope everything's okay with you. Thank you for being such a dear and wonderful friend to me last year. I know now that what we had was friendship more than anything else, but it was a great time for me, and I'll never forget all the good things we did together.

Write soon.

Love,
Diana

Diane mailed the letter the next morning and kept her fingers crossed that Jed would answer quickly. Until she knew what was troubling Caitlin she couldn't begin to help her.

The following day she found an unexpected ally. Dr. Westlake had been stopping by her room just to say hello whenever he was on the floor. She liked the doctor. He was friendly and really seemed to care about her. That day as he stuck his head around the doorway of the room, Diana was just getting out of her bed to sit in the chair by the window. She'd been lucky that the bed beside hers was still empty, and she had the room to herself.

"Here, let me help you." Dr. Westlake came forward and took her arm as she stood beside the bed. "You going to take a little jog around the hospital?" he teased.

Diana laughed. "Not yet, but I *am* feeling good."

"Good, that's what we like to hear."

"I was just going to sit over by the window."

"Beautiful day for it." He continued lightly supporting her elbow as she walked over to the chair by the window. When she was settled, he pulled up a chair opposite her and sat down himself.

Diana smiled at him. "I can't believe how well I feel," she said. "I feel like a whole new person."

"Karen's been wonderful for you." Dr. Westlake paused and fingered his chin. "What do you know about her?"

"What do you mean?"

"Well, has she told you anything about herself— how she comes to have such a talent for nursing?"

"No," Diana said cautiously. "She doesn't talk about herself much."

"Mmmm. I was curious and checked her records at the volunteer office. There was no mention of previous volunteer or hospital experience."

Diana swallowed. Should she tell him what she'd discovered about Karen Martin? Thinking she could trust him, she made a quick decision.

"Dr. Westlake," she said a little uncertainly. "I think I should tell you something. But please, don't say anything to Karen—or anyone else." She took a breath. "Karen isn't really who she says she is."

"Oh?"

"I didn't recognize her at first, but I'm sure now that she's a girl I went to school with. I don't know why, but she's disguising herself. I haven't said anything to her, and I don't think she's guessed that I know the truth, but for some reason she's trying to make me get better—and she doesn't want me to know who she is. I think she's really unhappy about something—that she's suffered as much as I have."

"Who is she?"

"Her name's Caitlin Ryan. We went to Highgate together. When I was there she was the prettiest and most popular girl in the school."

The doctor seemed almost stunned. "Ryan, you said?"

Diana nodded.

"Highgate? The private school down near Middletown?"

"Yes. I was there on scholarship. Caitlin wasn't, of course. She's rich—most of the kids are. I was invited out to her grandmother's place one weekend. It was incredible—stables and tennis courts and a swimming pool and a huge, huge house. I felt terribly out of place. I didn't ride or play tennis. I was never sure why she invited me."

Dr. Westlake stared disbelievingly at Diana. "What is her grandmother's name? Do you know?"

"Oh, sure. Everyone's heard of her grandmother. She's Regina Ryan. She owns Ryan Mining."

The doctor's face had gone white.

"What's the matter?" Diana cried. "You're not going to make her leave the hospital, are you?"

"No, no." Dr. Westlake laid a comforting hand

on Diana's shoulder. "I'm not about to make her leave."

"You won't tell her I told you?"

"I won't say a word to her, but I think we should try to find out why she's disguising herself. Tell me a little more about her. How old is she? Where do her parents live?"

"She's my age—sixteen—and her parents are dead, I think. That's why she lives with her grandmother."

"Dead?" Dr. Westlake's face paled again. "Are you sure?"

"I think so. I was never close friends with her at school, but everyone there knew about Caitlin. Her father had been killed in an accident or something, and her mother died when she was born."

Dr. Westlake pressed his fingers to his forehead and closed his eyes for an instant. "It can't be," he said almost under his breath. Then he seemed to pull himself together. "Do you know of anything that might have happened at school or at her home that would make her come to work here under an assumed name?"

"It might have something to do with me. Last fall when I was at Highgate . . ." Diana began describing to the doctor the terrible events—Ian Foster's accidental poisoning, her leaving the school, her relationship with Jed. "But after I left," she finished, "I just avoided everyone I'd known there. I only found out from a friend who came to see me here at the hospital that Jed and Caitlin started going together after I left Highgate. They were together all the time right up to the end of school. I heard that Caitlin was helping Ian Foster, too." Diana's voice broke, and she blinked a tear from her eye. "But then something must have happened—something to do with Jed, I think. When I mentioned his name to her the other day, she looked like she was going to cry. I wrote to him just the other day, asking him what had happened."

The doctor nodded. "That was a good idea. Will you let me know when you hear?"

"Yes."

"In the meantime, I'll do a little investigating on my own. I want you to stop worrying. I won't say anything to Caitlin. Perhaps she'll decide to confide in you."

"I don't know. I thought of telling her that I recognize her."

"Wait a bit before you do that. Whatever her reasons are for pretending she's someone else, she'd probably be pretty upset if she suspected you'd seen through her disguise. I'll come by and talk to you tomorrow."

"Thanks, Dr. Westlake. I hope you don't mind that I told you all this."

"I'm glad you told me, Diana—very glad." But Diana had no way of knowing the profound impact of the news she had given Dr. Westlake.

14

Gordon Westlake was stunned. Although he was careful not to let his emotions show to Diana, as soon as he was in the hallway, he let out a painful sigh and rubbed his hands across his eyes.

So Caitlin Ryan was Regina Ryan's granddaughter. No wonder she'd reminded him so much of Laura! Caitlin might very well be Laura's daughter. In fact, she *had* to be—he knew that Laura had been an only child.

Then he remembered the rest of what Diana had told him—that both of Caitlin's parents were dead. *Oh, God*, he thought, *Laura dead?* Even after all the years that had passed, the idea brought him a stabbing pain. She'd died in childbirth, Diana had said. Of course, Diana could be wrong—she admitted that she'd only learned about Caitlin's background second-hand.

One thing was certain—he wanted some answers. Something was terribly wrong in Caitlin Ryan's life at the moment or she would not be at the hospital in disguise. He made up his mind. He was going to pay Regina Ryan a visit.

He checked his watch. It was eleven in the morning. Two other doctors were on call, so he could leave the hospital for a few hours. When he reached his private office, he called directory assistance for the number of Regina Ryan. He was almost surprised to find it was listed.

Impatiently he dialed the number.

"Ryan residence."

"Yes, I'd like to speak to Regina Ryan."

"She's not here at the moment. May I take a message?"

"When do you expect her?"

"Not until this evening. May I ask who's calling?"

"Yes, Dr. Gordon Westlake. Do you know where I can reach her?"

"She's at the Ryan Mining offices, Dr. Westlake. If you'll leave your number, I'll be happy to have her return your call this evening."

"No, no need. I'll try to reach her there."

He dialed directory assistance again but then hung up. Why warn Regina that he was coming? She might very well avoid seeing him. He'd go directly to the mine offices and confront her. He knew where they were. He'd been there once years ago with Laura, although even then, Regina had made him feel unwelcome.

He told his secretary that he'd be gone for several hours and to notify the other doctors on call. Then, a look of determination on his handsome face, headed for the hospital parking lot. The meeting with Regina Ryan was long overdue.

* * *

Regina Ryan was in her mahogany paneled office going through some paperwork on her desk when her secretary announced a visitor.

"Dr. Westlake doesn't have an appointment," her secretary advised, "but he said it was urgent that he see you."

Regina nodded. "Very well. Show him in, but only for a moment."

As Gordon Westlake stepped forward into the office, he couldn't help noticing the contrast between the elegant, carpeted interior and the sordidness of the mine works outside. "Well, hello, Mrs. Ryan." He extended his hand.

She shook his hand. "What can I do to help you, Dr. Westlake? I don't believe we've met before."

"We have, but it was years ago."

"Oh? Are you with the environmentalists?" she asked.

"No, I'm here on personal business. May I?" He indicated the chair facing her desk.

"Of course."

He went right to the point. "I've had occasion to meet your granddaughter Caitlin recently."

"Have you?"

"Yes, she's been volunteering at Meadow Valley Hospital. I'm the director there."

Dr. Westlake didn't miss the amazed expression on Regina Ryan's face.

"You must be mistaken," she said in a moment. "My granddaughter does no volunteering."

Dr. Westlake gave her a wry smile. "I thought

you might not be aware of it. She's been disguising herself and using an assumed name."

He had Regina Ryan's full attention now. He continued. "One of the patients she's working with recognized her—they attended Highgate Academy together. Your granddaughter is very unhappy, Mrs. Ryan. I came here to find out why."

"I fail to see what business of yours her happiness is."

"I feel I have a distant personal interest. You obviously don't recognize me, but I knew your daughter, Laura, very well. We were engaged to each other in college, Mrs. Ryan. Do you remember me now?"

Despite her shock, Regina Ryan looked Gordon Westlake in the eye. "Yes, of course—the young medical student."

"I learned from the girl who recognized Caitlin that her parents are dead. Is this true?"

"Yes, my daughter is dead." Regina Ryan's voice was tight. "She died giving birth to Caitlin."

"I see." Dr. Westlake felt his heart constrict as his worst fear was confirmed. His Laura was dead. But as he looked at Regina Ryan's face, he saw there was pain there, too—along with bitterness. "I'm sorry. I'd—I'd hoped the girl was wrong.

"I never knew," he continued in a moment, forcing himself to speak in a level tone despite the pain he was feeling, "why Laura left me so suddenly. She told me it was because she thought I was seeing other women. I don't think she really believed that. I never was, you know."

"It's in the past, I no longer remember what her

reasons were," Mrs. Ryan said in a clipped tone. "She broke the engagement, and we went to Europe for an extended visit."

"And that's where she met Caitlin's father?"

"No, Dr. Westlake, it is not."

"But if Caitlin is sixteen, Laura must have married right after she broke off our engagement," he reasoned.

Regina studied him, then smiled coldly. "Really, Dr. Westlake, you're an intelligent man—I never faulted you for that. I thought you would have put two and two together by now."

Gordon Westlake sat bolt upright in his chair. "You mean Caitlin is my daughter?"

"Yes. When we reached Europe I discovered that I hadn't taken Laura away in time. She was already pregnant with your child."

"Why didn't you tell me? Why? I would have married her. I had a right to know!"

"Because my daughter wanted to have nothing to do with you."

"I don't believe you!"

"Believe what you wish. After Laura died, I raised the child. She has turned out very well."

"She thinks I'm dead, too."

"I believe she's told people that, to make things easier, but I told her that her father had deserted her."

Dr. Westlake was enraged. "But that was a lie!"

Regina Ryan shrugged slightly. "I made the best of a bad situation. No more, no less."

Dr. Westlake rose; began pacing in front of Mrs. Ryan's desk, trying to still the turmoil he was feeling. He had a daughter—Caitlin. All these years, he'd never known. He turned to Regina Ryan. "I'm going to speak to Caitlin and tell her the truth!"

"Do as you wish," she said coolly. "I will make no attempt to stop you. However, I wonder if her reaction will be what you expect. She has been quite content living with me."

"I'd appreciate your saying nothing to Caitlin about this until I've had a chance to speak to her."

"Very well, but I will expect you to inform her that this little escapade of hers is over. She's had her bit of rebellion, but the volunteer staff at a hospital is no place for a Ryan."

"I think I'm beginning to understand why she went to such lengths to cover up her identity!"

"Do you really? If I were you, I would not jump to conclusions." She picked up her pen. "Well, I am a busy woman. If there is nothing else—"

"Is that all you have to say?"

"What did you expect? I am not pleased you came, but since you did, the expedient thing to do was to tell you the truth. Now that I have, I have no further business with you."

"You're a cold woman."

"I do what I have to do," she said firmly. "Good day, Dr. Westlake."

Gordon Westlake was furious all during the drive back from Ryan Mining. Regina Ryan hadn't changed: She still was a heartless, power-driven woman. Angrily he thought of all the lost years when he could have been standing beside his daughter, helping her grow, giving her the love she so obviously wasn't getting from her grandmother. But it wasn't too late. He would talk to Caitlin, and together they would try to make up for lost time.

To think that this beautiful young woman was his daughter—his and Laura's. . . .

bo

15

Watching Diana improve so rapidly over the last weeks had given Caitlin a warm feeling. But it wasn't enough. Helping Diana would never be enough to ease the guilt that she still felt. She knew that now. She had to tell Diana the truth—that she herself had left the shed door unlocked. Her secret had done enough damage. It was time to end it.

As Caitlin parked her car at the hospital that afternoon and started walking toward the building, she composed the words she would say to Diana. It was going to be awful. Diana had become her friend, but when she heard the truth and found out how much she'd suffered needlessly all because of Caitlin, she might turn on her. But Caitlin couldn't let that stop her from doing what she knew was right; it was a chance she had to take.

Caitlin changed into her uniform. Then she walked determinedly into Diana's room. But Diana wasn't alone. Laurence Baxter was with her.

"Oh, hi, Karen," Diana called cheerfully, making Caitlin feel even worse. "Look what Laurence brought me." She held up a soft pink blouse under her chin. The color brought out the new rosiness in Diana's cheeks. "Laurence thinks I'm getting ready to leave the hospital pretty soon."

"And why not?" Laurence asked, smiling.

"It sounds silly," Diana said more seriously, "but I'm going to miss this place—especially you, Karen."

Caitlin felt as if she were choking. "I'll miss you, too, but we don't have to stop being friends."

"Yeah, I know, but I think I'm going to be leaving Virginia. My father brought me some application papers yesterday to a school in Pennsylvania. He doesn't think I'll have any problem getting accepted."

"You're leaving Virginia?" Caitlin couldn't contain the surprise in her voice.

"It probably would be better." Diana smiled. "I'll get a whole new start."

Laurence was studying Caitlin's face, and she felt as if her terrible secret was written all over it. She couldn't think of what to say. Finally she blurted out. "I was going to bring you some juice, but I left it at the nurses' stand. Let me go get it."

The juice had been an excuse, of course, but what was she going to do now? she wondered. Laurence would probably stay with Diana for a while. She'd have to wait until tomorrow to talk to Diana. Yes, tomorrow, she promised herself. She'd make sure they had some time alone tomorrow.

* * *

Early that evening Diana picked up the receiver on her bedside table. "Hello?"

"Hello, Diana. It's Jed."

"Oh, Jed!" Diana sat up in her bed. "It's good to hear from you. How are you?"

"Not bad. How about *you*?"

"I'm feeling much better."

"Good. I've been worried about you."

"You got my letter?"

"Yeah. I got it today. I've got a lot to tell you. I should have told you this a while ago, but I didn't know how to get in touch with you." He paused. "I've been pretty messed up myself, trying to sort things out."

"Do you know why Caitlin's here?"

"I have a good idea. Listen, Diana, she may be helping you—and I give her credit for that—but I wouldn't go around feeling sorry for her."

"Why?"

"It's a long story."

"I'm not going anywhere, Jed," Diana said. "And I really need to know."

"Well, just before the end of school—the day before the prom, in fact—I was helping her move some stuff back home. I accidentally found a letter addressed to me. She'd written it right after you'd left school, but she'd never given it to me. It was a confession letter. She admitted being the one who'd left the Fosters' shed door unlocked so that Ian got into the poison. Oh, she didn't do it on purpose. But when the news came out about what had happened to Ian, she kept it a secret. She let *you* take the blame. She said she was afraid of losing me."

"No, I can't believe it," Diana whispered. Her shock at hearing the news was tempered by a strange feeling of relief at having part of the puzzle solved. It explained the words Caitlin had whispered to her when she was so sick.

"You'd better believe it. It's the truth. She's known all along what you were going through. But it wasn't in her best interest to take the blame for what she'd done. Her pretty little world would have been wrecked. So she let you suffer instead."

"But Laurence told me she's been helping Ian."

"Yeah, and, boy, did I admire her for that," Jed said with bitterness. "I know now that all she was doing was easing her own guilty conscience."

"No, Jed!"

"It's the truth, Diana."

"But she's done so much for me. She's spent hours and hours here. She's saved my life."

"You've got it backward. She's the one who almost destroyed it. Think of how she used to treat you. Think of how she tried to break us up!"

"But she's so unhappy, Jed. If you could see her! I know she's changed!"

"If she's changed so much, why hasn't she told you the truth?"

"I don't know. Maybe she's afraid. She thinks I believe she's Karen Martin. She needs to talk to someone, Jed. I know she misses you. What happened? What did you say to her?"

"Nothing. After I read the letter and found out how she'd been lying to me and using me, I was so angry I left. I haven't talked to her since, and I don't want to."

"No wonder she looks so miserable. You didn't even tell her why you left?"

"She didn't deserve it."

"But she loves you. I know she does!"

"That's her problem." Jed's tone was stubborn and angry. "Not yours."

"She's trying to prove herself," Diana said. "That's got to be why she's here. She's trying to make up for what she's done by trying to help me and Ian."

"She waited long enough," Jed spat out.

"Jed, don't you care about her at all anymore?"

There was a moment's silence on the other end of the phone.

"Jed?"

"Yes! I still care about her. I hate myself because I can't stop thinking about her."

"Then write to her. Or call her."

"Are you crazy? Maybe I still think about her, but I'll never forgive her."

"I've forgiven her," Diana said quietly.

There was another moment's silence on Jed's end of the phone. "She doesn't deserve knowing someone as good as you," he said finally.

"Are you going back to Highgate in the fall?"

"Probably, but that won't change anything between Caitlin and me. I don't want to have anything to do with her anymore."

"You won't spread it around about Caitlin being to blame, will you?"

"I'd love to! Why should she get away with it? But I won't—not unless you start getting hurt by it again."

"Thanks, Jed."

"Why are you doing this for her?" Jed sounded truly puzzled.

"Because I think she knows how wrong she's been, and I think she'll decide to tell everyone the truth herself."

"I hope you're right." He sighed. "Listen, keep in touch with me, Diana. Don't pull another disappearing act like you did last year."

"I won't. I don't have reason to anymore. Whether you want to hear it or not, I'll write and let you know what happens. And thanks for calling, Jed. I know you're pretty unhappy, too."

"I'll get over it. Call Emily, will you? I know she'd like to hear from you."

"I will, tomorrow. Good night, Jed."

"Good night."

After Diana hung up the phone, she leaned back on her pillows. When the terrible accident had happened, she was sure she hadn't been to blame. But since it appeared that she had been the last person to close the shed door, everyone had blamed her. And after a while she had believed it herself. Caitlin's telling her she wasn't to blame had helped bring her out of her severe depression, but still, Diana had been left with lingering doubts. Now, finally, it all made sense. What a relief it was to know she hadn't been responsible for Ian's plight. She felt as if a huge burden had been lifted from her shoulders!

But now Caitlin was feeling that burden. Diana wanted to help her, but she couldn't—not until

Caitlin told her the truth on her own . . . if she ever did.

The next afternoon Caitlin kept her promise. Although her stomach felt tight from nervousness and fear, she knew she couldn't keep her secret to herself any longer. She went to Diana's room as usual, and as the two girls sat beside each other facing the windows and the view of the rolling green hills beyond, she silently rehearsed the words she would say. Diana had opened a magazine and was flipping through it, but Caitlin sat with her hands gripping the arms of her chair.

"Diana," she finally said hesitantly, "there's something I have to tell you. I know I should have said this a long time ago—but I was afraid." Diana looked over to her, and Caitlin swallowed and took a deep breath. "Diana, I'm not Karen Martin. I'm Caitlin—Caitlin Ryan." She rushed on. "I know it was awful of me to pretend I was someone else, but I wanted to help you *so* much, and it seemed—"

"I know, Caitlin," Diana said calmly.

"You know!"

"I recognized you, and so did Laurence. We didn't say anything because we thought you had a reason for doing what you're doing."

It took Caitlin a minute to digest what Diana was telling her. "I do have a reason, Diana." She looked down at her hands to build up her courage, then plunged on. "That's what I wanted to tell you today. It goes back to the accident and Ian. I'm so, so sorry I didn't tell you sooner. I've caused so much pain and hurt. I've been a terrible person for not telling the truth, but I can't keep it inside any longer. I'm the one who left the shed unlocked. I didn't do it on purpose. I was getting a prop for the fund-raiser. I was so worried about you and Jed being inside the Fosters' house together that I forgot to lock the shed when I left. You see, I was jealous of you. I wanted Jed, but he never looked at anyone but you. I didn't find out what had happened to Ian until I read the article in the paper. I knew you were taking the blame, but I was afraid to tell everyone the truth. After you left Highgate, I thought it wouldn't matter anymore. But I was wrong. I never stopped feeling guilty, and a month later I wrote a letter to Jed telling him the truth. But I never gave it to him. We were going together by then, and I was afraid I'd lose him."

Caitlin buried her face in her hands. "I've lost him anyway now. I think he found out. The night of the prom he was acting strangely, and the next day he was gone. I haven't heard from him since." Caitlin's voice trembled. "It was then I knew I had to help you, to try to undo all the wrong I'd done. I'd tried to help Ian, too, but he went off to a special school for the summer. So I thought this up and came to the hospital. I thought maybe it would be better if I helped you without letting you know it was me. But that wasn't enough either. I can't let you go on blaming yourself for something you didn't do!"

Diana put her hand on Caitlin's arm. "It's okay. Go ahead and cry."

"You must hate me!"

"No, I don't hate you. I've forgiven you."

"But it was my own fault. You've been so sick. Your whole life was almost ruined—all because of me!" Caitlin removed her glasses and wiped away the tears that were running down her cheeks, streaking her makeup. She set the glasses on the windowsill. She wouldn't need them anymore. "I know what I have to do. I'm going to go to the Fosters and everyone else and tell them the truth. I'll make sure that everyone on campus knows that I was the one responsible."

Diana shook her head. "Don't do that, Caitlin. What difference would it make now? I have a whole new life. It doesn't matter what they think of me. I'm not going back to Highgate, but you are."

"I'd never feel good about myself again unless I did," Caitlin argued.

"You've told me the truth. That's all that matters to me."

Caitlin sat silently for a moment, her hands clenched in her lap. In a moment she looked up. "Why are you being so good to me?"

"Because I think you're really unhappy, and something makes me feel that it goes beyond the accident. It's Jed, isn't it?"

At Diana's sympathetic tone, Caitlin sighed. "I love him so much, Diana. But more importantly, he's the only person who ever cared about me. I feel so empty now."

"But you have your grandmother."

Caitlin snorted. "I don't tell many people, but I don't think she's ever loved me."

"Why?" Diana asked.

The words just poured out. "I think she blames me for my mother's death," Caitlin admitted. "My mother was her only child, and from stuff my grandmother said, I don't think she ever got over losing her so young. Sometimes she forgets and says things like, 'If things had been different, Laura would be on the board of the mine now.' Then she'll give me this strange look. She never even hugs me, and as soon as I was old enough, I was sent off to boarding school. And my father's no better. He didn't die, like I tell everyone—oh, maybe he's dead now—but he abandoned me after my mother died. He's never tried to see me or get in touch with me."

"You've *never* seen your father?"

"I don't even know who he is. My grandmother wouldn't tell me, and after a while, I stopped asking. I don't care anymore. I hate him for what he did to me. Then I met Jed, and everything seemed so good for a while. But now I've lost him, too!" Caitlin let out a little sob. "I'm sure he doesn't want anything to do with me anymore."

"He may change his mind." Diana paused thoughtfully as if trying to make up her mind. "I talked to him. He knows what happened—he found your letter the day before the prom. He's angry and bitter, but I think he still loves you. I told him that *I* forgave you and that he should, too."

"He found the letter," Caitlin whispered the confirmation almost to herself. Now she was more sure than ever that Jed hated her. If he'd been

159

ready to forgive her, he wouldn't have run off as he had. He would have tried to talk to her.

She shook her head sadly. "It's over. I—I guess I just have to get used to the idea."

"Don't give up hope," Diana pleaded. "He needs time. Oh, Caitlin, he's just hurt. He thinks you deliberately lied to him and used him. I know you didn't, and someday he'll realize that, too. Write to him—tell him you've told me—tell him how sorry you are. Tell him about your grandmother."

"I don't think it will do any good. I *did* keep the truth from him. And he knows about my grandmother."

"Then I'll write to him and explain how awful you feel."

"No." Caitlin shook her head firmly. "Too much has happened—too much has gone wrong. I have to forget him. I have to, Diana." Caitlin sighed. "It's time I started making a new life, too."

Diana didn't argue further. Smiling sadly she told Caitlin, "Whatever you decide, I'll help you."

"You're a good friend, Diana. Thanks."

When Caitlin walked out into the hall an hour later, she felt free of her burden of guilt for the first time in months. Now she was determined to put her own past behind her, just as Diana was doing, and start over.

She didn't see Laurence Baxter approaching down the hall until he called her name. "Caitlin, do you have a second? I'd like to talk to you."

She nodded. "Sure, Laurence." The fact that he'd called her by her real name didn't surprise her. After what Diana had told her, she realized Laurence had recognized her days before.

He led her to the side of the hall.

"Listen, Caitlin," he said quietly. "I didn't mean to eavesdrop, but I heard part of what you said to Diana. I admire you for telling her the truth. I know how hard it must have been for you."

"There's nothing admirable about it. I should have done it a long time ago, Laurence."

"We all make mistakes. Try to think of the good side. If it wasn't for you, Diana still might be fading away."

"And if it wasn't for me, she wouldn't have gotten sick in the first place."

"Don't be too hard on yourself. If Diana forgives you, that's all that counts. Besides," he added lightly, "you can stop wearing all that makeup now."

"The rest of the hospital staff might wonder."

"I'll tell them Diana and I did a makeover on you," he said and laughed.

Caitlin smiled at him, then grew serious. "I was sure that when I went in there today and told her what I'd done, she'd end up hating me, too. Instead, she wants to be my friend."

"So do I."

Caitlin stared at him.

"I know a little about what's happened with you and Jed," Laurence added quietly. "I know you still hurt, but I like the way you've given up everything to help Diana." He hesitated. "I guess what I'm trying to say is that I'd like to get to know you better—if you'd like it, that is."

Caitlin was stunned. It was the last thing she expected Laurence to say. Not that she'd ever thought he disliked her. He was nice-looking and smart, but they'd been involved with different groups at school and apparently never had much in common. Of course, that was before Caitlin had changed so much.

"I'd like that, too," she said finally. "But are you sure?"

"I'm positive." He grinned. "My parents' place isn't too far from your grandmother's. Would you like to go to the movies one night this week?"

"Well, fine. That would be great."

"How about Friday night?"

"All right." She nodded, still a little amazed. "Do you know how to get to my grandmother's?"

"Everyone knows where Ryan Acres is. Is six-thirty okay? We can go to the early show and then get something to eat."

"I'll be ready." For an instant her eyes grew sad. "I wish we could take Diana, too. I hate to leave her alone in the hospital every night now that she's getting stronger."

"I've got a lot of things planned for Diana when she's better, but this time let's just get to know each other."

Caitlin nodded and smiled as she looked up at Laurence's face. He had such warm brown eyes. In fact she was feeling warmed all over that both he and Diana had forgiven her. She'd lost Jed, the only true love in her life, but she still had friends. She *could* start over again.

16

"Karen?" Dr. Westlake met Caitlin as she stepped into the hall from the volunteers' room just as she was ready to leave. "How are you today?"

"Just fine, Dr. Westlake." Caitlin smiled.

"Could you come into my office for a minute? I'd like to talk to you."

Caitlin hesitated. "I'm in a bit of a hurry."

"I won't take long," he said. "And it's important."

The doctor was smiling, so she didn't think anything was wrong. He probably wanted to talk about Diana's progress. "Okay," she agreed.

Dr. Westlake led her past his secretary's desk, through a door at the back of the room, and into his private office. It was simply but tastefully decorated, with wooden bookshelves lining the walls and one large window behind his desk overlooking the rolling hills beyond.

"Have a seat." Dr. Westlake smiled. He went around the desk and took a seat in his own chair. "I saw Diana this morning. She's doing remarkably well."

"Yes, she is, isn't she?"

"You can be proud of what you've done."

"I guess I am."

"I think you've got a real talent, and I hope you'll decide to make use of it someday. But that's not what I brought you here to talk about."

He leaned his arms on his desk. His eyes were on Caitlin's face, and there was a glowing warmth in them. Caitlin couldn't quite interpret the look. It reminded her of the loving way Jed had gazed at her from time to time.

"This is a difficult subject for me to broach," Dr. Westlake continued, "so please be patient with me."

A difficult subject? What did that mean? Wasn't he happy with her work? Had he discovered she wasn't really Karen Martin? Was he going to tell her she had to leave? The hospital was the only comforting place in her life now. She certainly had felt no happiness at Ryan Acres recently. Especially the night before. Her grandmother had been behaving oddly. She hadn't said anything to her, but Regina Ryan had watched Caitlin as though expecting at any minute to catch her doing something wrong. Caitlin was desperately afraid that her grandmother had found out she was sneaking off to the hospital every day.

Dr. Westlake was speaking again, and Caitlin brought her thoughts back to the present. "I had a long talk with Diana yesterday," he said quietly. "I was asking about you. I was curious. You reminded me so very much of a woman I loved and almost married many years ago. I wondered if

ou'd talked at all about yourself. After some
probing on my part, Diana admitted—and please
don't be angry with her for this—that she recognized you as a girl she'd gone to school with. She
said your name was Caitlin Ryan—"

"Dr. Westlake," Caitlin interrupted, "please, I
can explain. I didn't mean to lie to anyone, but it
was so important!"

He held up his hand to silence her. "Wait, let me
finish. I'm not going to fire you, if that's what
you're afraid of. The name Ryan startled me, that's
all. Then Diana told me that you were the granddaughter of Regina Ryan." Dr. Westlake cleared his
throat.

Caitlin waited in dread.

"I knew your grandmother a long time ago. And
I knew your mother very well." There was a flash
of pain on his face. "I decided I had to go talk to
your grandmother to find out why you'd disguised
yourself to work in this hospital and help a friend. I
suspected there was some deep unhappiness in
your life. Diana intimated as much. She said that
she'd been told both your parents were dead."

"Yes," Caitlin said quietly, her hands gripping
the arms of her chair.

Dr. Westlake seemed to flinch, but he continued
quickly. "I met with your grandmother yesterday,
and what she told me left me stunned."

"I'm sorry," Caitlin burst in, "really sorry. I only
wanted to help Diana. I didn't mean to cause
trouble. Oh, God, I've made such a mess of
things!"

"No, no, wait. I'm not angry with you, and you

haven't caused trouble. Your coming to the hospital as Karen Martin was a blessing in disguise—in more ways than one. As I said before, I knew your mother, Laura, very well. While we were in college and I was finishing up my medical studies, we fell in love. We got engaged and planned our wedding for the next fall. She was going to work while I completed my internship. Then something happened—to this day I don't know exactly what—except that she wrote me just before graduation saying that she wanted nothing else to do with me.

"Caitlin, I loved your mother as I've loved no other woman since. I could only guess that your grandmother made Laura believe lies about me. She wanted someone better than a poor medical student for her daughter.

"I tried to get in touch with Laura, but she and her mother had left Virginia. No one would tell me where they'd gone. For months and months I kept trying to find her. Finally I gave up, realizing she didn't want me anymore."

"Why are you telling me this?" Caitlin said with alarm. His mention of her mother had brought her terrible, unexpected pain.

"There's a reason. Let me finish." His eyes were soft and filled with sympathy as he looked at her. "When I went to talk to your grandmother the other day, I assumed that Laura had married someone else after she left me, and that you were the daughter of that marriage." He took a deep breath.

"Caitlin, I know this is going to come as a shock to you. I'm your father."

Caitlin stared at him. Her mouth dropped open. he couldn't have heard him correctly—she buldn't have!

"Your grandmother told me that she'd never told ou who your father was. That was wrong of her— *otally* wrong of her! To add to it, I've never known had a daughter. Neither of them told me that your nother was pregnant with you. I would have narried her—it was all I wanted in the world. I idn't know until yesterday what had happened eventeen years ago. I didn't know until then, ither, that your mother had died in childbirth."

"I don't believe you!"

"Caitlin, it's true."

"No!" Caitlin slammed her hands over her ears. No! You're lying!"

"I'm not! Does it upset you so much that I'm our father?" Dr. Westlake's face had gone pale.

"You abandoned me. She died, and you didn't vant me. My grandmother told me. You only vanted my mother's money. You didn't want a •aby!"

"That's not true!" Dr. Westlake pushed his tall, thletic frame out of his chair, rushed around his lesk, and reached for Caitlin, who'd risen to her eet as well.

"You can say that now, but I don't believe you. ou never wanted me. I despise you! I hate you!"

"Caitlin, listen to me!" He dropped his hands onto her shoulders and pleaded with her. "I never leserted you. I just didn't know!"

Caitlin backed free of his hands and glared at him. "I don't want to hear anything else you have

to say. You should have come to me a long time ago
when I used to lie awake at night and long for a
father who loved me. I don't need you anymore!"

Before Dr. Westlake could say another word,
Caitlin ran from his office, past his startled secretary, and down the hall.

He stood frozen, his hands still outstretched, his
handsome face bewildered and full of pain. He
started after her, then stopped. He wanted to
follow her, but what more could he say now? It was
obvious to him she was in shock.

For the moment he'd have to let Caitlin go. He
prayed only that as she had time to think, she'd
remember his words and reconsider. He wanted to
hold her and comfort her and tell her everything
was all right—that from now on he'd make up for
all those years they'd been separated. But he
couldn't do any of that until she was willing to
accept him.

He swung back toward his office. Ignoring the
curious look on his secretary's face, he shut the
door behind him, went to the phone on his desk,
and dialed the number of Ryan Mining.

"I'd like to speak to Regina Ryan," he said
abruptly to the receptionist.

"I'm sorry. She left early today."

Dr. Westlake hung up the phone without saying
good-bye, then dialed the Ryan residence.

Rollins answered the phone and when Dr. Westlake asked for Mrs. Ryan, Rollins said, "She's busy
at the moment. Who's calling?"

"Dr. Westlake, and tell her I must speak to her.
It's urgent!"

In a moment Regina Ryan's voice came through the receiver. "Hello, Dr. Westlake."

"You knew, didn't you?" he burst out. "You knew before I left your office what kind of a response I'd get from my daughter."

"I told you, Gordon," Regina Ryan answered calmly, "to do as you wished. I made no promises about how she would react."

"What kind of poisonous lies have you been feeding her? She talked of my having wanted her mother's money, not her."

"Children exaggerate. Perhaps that's the image she's had of it."

"That line won't work with me," he growled. "You're a fool, Regina. You've hated me and have never forgiven me for winning your daughter's love and trying to take her away from you. Now you're carrying out your revenge through your granddaughter, but it's going to backfire in your face."

"Really, Gordon, I think you're getting carried away. I seek no revenge, and I seriously doubt Caitlin is unhappy."

As Regina spoke, Dr. Westlake looked out the window of his office and saw Caitlin leaving the hospital building and running toward her car.

"She's leaving the hospital now," he said brusquely. "She seems very upset. I'd advise you not to leave your house. She's going to need someone!"

He slammed the phone down and pounded his fist on his desk. *Damn Regina Ryan*, he thought to himself. *Damn her!*

* * *

Caitlin could barely see through her tears as she raced toward her little red sports car, pulled the door open, and slid inside. Her fingers trembled as she inserted the key in the ignition.

How could it be? How could Dr. Westlake be her *father*? And how could he dare come to her now and tell her that? After all the time when he'd made no effort, why had he chosen now? And to lie to her as he had—to try to convince her that he hadn't deliberately abandoned her!

Caitlin's car screeched out of the hospital parking lot and swung out down the side road that led to the main highway. As if on automatic pilot, she headed south to Ryan Acres.

What was she to do? She'd thought he was so kind and good; she'd trusted him and admired him as director of the hospital. But now that she knew the truth, she never wanted to see him again.

Yet the fact remained. Caitlin Ryan, who'd grown up an orphan, now had a father. She just couldn't believe that after all the years of wondering what he was like, she'd met the man who hadn't even been a name to her. Just knowing who he was, what he looked like, what he did for a living, made her feel suddenly more like other kids who'd always known their fathers. But what could she say about her father? That he'd just appeared out of nowhere? That he'd done wonderful things and become a success, while he'd left her to face life on her own since she was a baby? That now that she was old enough not to need constant care, he'd come back!

She took a corner too quickly, almost ran the car into a ditch, swung the wheel, and sat up straighter. She forced herself to pay more attention to her driving. *Oh, Jed . . . Jed,* she cried silently. *If only you were here—if only you still loved me—you'd know what to do. Please come back . . . please help me! I feel so alone!*

But Caitlin knew he wouldn't be back. She had to do this alone. She was growing a little calmer. Her hands were no longer gripping the steering wheel so tightly that her knuckles showed white. She took several long, deep breaths.

She'd done the right thing, though, in walking out of Dr. Westlake's office. He'd wanted her to understand, and she'd rejected him, just as he'd rejected her. He deserved it!

As she neared Ryan Acres, her thoughts turned to Regina Ryan. Caitlin figured she'd be angry now that the man who claimed to be her father had told her about the volunteer work at the hospital. Caitlin could almost see her grandmother's scowls and hear her terse remarks—and her questions about Dr. Westlake. Her grandmother's behavior the day before made sense now. She'd known already that Caitlin was spending her time at the hospital instead of at the club. She'd seen Dr. Westlake and talked to him. She must have known that he would then talk to Caitlin. Why hadn't her grandmother said anything? Why?

Caitlin chewed her lip as she stared straight ahead at the road. There wouldn't be any warmth or loving back at Ryan Acres either. But it was the only place she had to go to, and Regina Ryan was the only person she could count on. At least her grandmother, despite her lack of warmth, had stood beside her, fed her, clothed her, cared for her, and given her the best of everything. Her father hadn't done one thing for her.

The shattering events of the afternoon made Caitlin dizzy all over again. At the thought of her father, she grew angry and pressed her foot harder on the gas pedal.

Why would he have chosen now, when her life was torn and confused, to announce himself? What did he think he had to gain? The questions gnawed at her all the way home.

17

Her grandmother was waiting for her in the living room when Caitlin rushed through the front doors and into the elegant entrance hall.

"You're late," Regina said before Caitlin had a chance to utter a word. Yet there was no reprimand in her grandmother's words. She seemed cool and collected. "Did your father keep you at the hospital?"

On top of all that had happened that day, Caitlin was too numb to register surprise at her grandmother's words.

"I don't know what's gotten into you, dear." Her grandmother sighed. "First, that Foster boy, now running off to play nursemaid at a hospital. There's no need for a Ryan to involve herself in those concerns. I thought you knew better."

Caitlin hardly paid attention to her grandmother's gentle rebuke. "Why didn't you tell me you'd seen him? Why didn't you tell me who he was and warn me?" she cried.

Mrs. Ryan stepped closer, a concerned look on her face. "I had no idea your paths had crossed at the hospital until he came to see me. And you can imagine what a shock that was after all these years! He asked me not to interfere.''

"You still should have told me!"

"From what he said to me, he was absolutely sure you would accept him. I don't know how wise that is, my dear.''

"I didn't, Grandmother! I didn't even know who he was until he called me into his office this afternoon when I was leaving.''

Mrs. Ryan lifted her brows. "And have you two now made a reconciliation?''

"How could I do that? He abandoned me. He's never tried to see me! He tried to tell me today that he didn't even know I'd been born. I didn't believe him, of course!''

"No, there's no reason to. He's grasping at straws, dear. He's grown successful and suddenly has regrets about what he left behind.''

"It's true, Grandmother, isn't it, that he deserted me?''

Mrs. Ryan came forward and took Caitlin's arm. "You're tired and hungry, and it's no time to dwell on these painful things. Margaret's laid a table for us in the small sitting room. It will be much more cozy in there. We'll eat and then we'll talk. You need to calm down.''

The cornish hen, wild rice and Caesar salad Margaret eventually placed before them looked delicious, but Caitlin's appetite failed her. Feeling dazed, she only picked at her food while her grandmother chattered on about that day's inspection by the Bureau of Mines. Caitlin knew that the older woman was trying to distract her from the confusion and painful thoughts in her mind, but it was so difficult to put them aside.

Regina didn't bring up the subject of Dr. Westlake again until they were finishing their blueberry torte. "I know this has been a terribly trying day for you," she said quietly, "but do try to put this unpleasant episode with your father out of your thoughts. It does no good to dwell on it."

"I know, Grandmother."

"I shall see that he brings you no unhappiness in the future." Regina patted Caitlin's hand. "Why don't you go up to bed now? You're exhausted. A good night's sleep will do wonders for you."

Responding to her grandmother's sympathetic tone, Caitlin nodded. "Yes, I think I will. Good night, Grandmother, and thank you."

Still, even as Caitlin climbed between the sheets, she felt little peace. Eventually she did fall asleep, firm in her resolution to reject Dr. Gordon Westlake as her father, just as he'd rejected her.

The following morning Caitlin debated about going to the hospital. She was afraid to run the risk of seeing Dr. Westlake, but she had to see Diana. She couldn't just go off without saying good-bye.

At first her grandmother refused to let her go, but after Caitlin assured her that her volunteering was over and that she just wanted to pick up some of her things, Mrs. Ryan reluctantly gave her permission.

"By the way," Mrs. Ryan called as Caitlin was

walking out the door, "Laurence Baxter called fo you last night after you'd gone to bed."

"Did he? Did he say what he wanted?"

"Only that he'd call again. We chatted a while His grandparents are old friends of mine. A very pleasant young man."

Caitlin nodded. She couldn't think of Laurence just then; she still felt too confused and upset by the events of the day before.

Caitlin parked her car away from the hospita and used one of the side entrances in order to avoid Dr. Westlake. As she stepped into the second floor hall, looking in both directions to be sure her father wasn't around, she saw Laurence standing just outside Diana's door.

Although Laurence's bright smile warmed her her thoughts were elsewhere. Unconsciously, she glanced over her shoulder to be sure Dr. Westlake hadn't appeared.

Laurence reached out and lightly touched her hand. "Did your grandmother tell you I called las night?"

"Yes, she did."

"She was really nice. We talked for a little while I didn't know it, but she knows my father and grandfather. They ride to the hunt together."

"She told me." She tried to focus her attention on what he was saying. She didn't want him wondering what was wrong with her, since she had no intention of telling *anyone* about Dr Westlake.

But he did notice. He frowned. "Is something wrong?"

Immediately she forced herself to think clearly. "Uh, no—well, actually, I'm kind of upset. Today will be my last day at the hospital. Grandmother wants me to spend some time at home the rest of the summer."

"Oh, really?" Laurence said with concern. "Diana will be disappointed."

"I know. I was just going to tell her. I feel pretty sad about it."

"She'll understand, and it doesn't mean you won't see her again. The reason I called last night," he explained, "was to tell you about the idea I had to surprise her."

"Oh?"

"Yes, a picnic. I thought the two of us could pack a lunch and drive Diana up to the state park next weekend. She wants to get out of here and get some fresh air."

"That sounds like a terrific idea." Caitlin was relieved to have something to think about besides herself, at least temporarily. She concentrated on the picnic plans. "I could bring some fried chicken—she likes that, doesn't she? And I'll even help Margaret bake a pie."

"Of course, I'll have to talk to Diana's doctors first," Laurence added. "But I don't think they'll mind."

"How will we surprise her?"

"Maybe one of us can take her for a drive, while the other sets up the picnic stuff."

Caitlin nodded. She was feeling nervous again about standing in the hall. "You can call me, and we can get the details straightened out."

"Or we can talk about it Friday night," he smiled. "We still have a date, don't we?"

"Sure we do. I haven't changed my mind."

"Good. I'll pick you up about six?"

Despite her nervousness, she smiled warmly to him. "Fine."

"I'd better let you go talk to Diana. I was just leaving." He took her hand and squeezed it gently. "I'll see you later."

As Laurence walked away from her down the hall, Caitlin pressed her fingertips to her cheeks. So much had happened in the past few days. Her life was changing so quickly she couldn't quite comprehend it all. But she felt that Laurence's arrival was definitely a positive addition. His steadiness and easygoing attitude were just what she needed right now. She turned and started toward Diana's room.

She didn't notice Dr. Westlake coming out of one of the rooms behind her. But he saw her and strode quickly up beside her.

"Caitlin," he pleaded, "I have to talk to you."

Startled, she stopped in her tracks, then started walking again.

"Please! You can at least hear me out, can't you? I was worried about your getting home all right last night. I asked your grandmother to call me."

Caitlin's expression turned hard. "I don't have anything to say to you."

"You can't let your grandmother convince you that I deserted you all those years ago. It's simply not true! What *I* told you yesterday was the truth!"

She refused to look up at him. "You lied to my grandmother, too. You lie to everybody."

"What are you talking about?"

"I don't want to have anything to do with you! Don't you understand that?" Caitlin was growing panicky. She didn't want Dr. Westlake following her into Diana's room and causing a scene. She didn't want anyone to know what a horrible father she had. She swung on her heel and started back toward the staircase.

"Where are you going?" he asked, turning and walking alongside her.

"I'm leaving!"

He stepped in front of her, started to put his hands on her shoulders, then stopped himself. "No, wait, Caitlin. I don't want you rushing out of the hospital the way you did yesterday. I won't say another word to you, but please think about what I told you. Look at *all* the facts carefully." For a moment he and Caitlin stared at each other.

There was so much pain and hurt written on Dr. Westlake's face that Caitlin averted her gaze. She wouldn't let him get to her. She saw no reason why she should trust him. If she started to believe in him, he'd let her down again and abandon her as he'd done before. She couldn't stand to go through that a second time. She wanted him to suffer— suffer as much as she had!

Without acknowledging him, she spun around and hurried toward Diana's room.

18

On Friday night when Laurence came to Rya
Acres to pick up Caitlin, Regina Ryan was her mos
cordial self. "I'm so delighted to meet you, Lau
rence," she greeted him warmly.

Laurence took her outstretched hand. "It's nic
to meet you, too, Mrs. Ryan."

"As a matter of fact," Mrs. Ryan continued, "
ran into your grandfather the other evening at
party. We had a lovely chat. With the hunt seaso
not far away, we should all get together for som
riding. The Weston Hunt/Chase is coming up i
late September."

"I'd like that," Laurence beamed, "though I'
have to get my legs back in shape. I didn't do muc
riding this spring."

"Oh? You were busy with your studies?"

"Laurence may apply early to Harvard," Caitli
put in.

"My, how impressive. Well, good luck to you."

"Thanks." Laurence looked a little embarrassed
It wasn't his style to brag about himself.

"Well, I'll let you two get off to your movie. If it'

not too late, stop in and have a snack with me when you return."

Caitlin gave her grandmother a quick look of surprise, but Laurence didn't know how unusual that suggestion was. In fact, Caitlin couldn't remember her grandmother ever having asked any of her boyfriends to come in after a first date.

"If it's not too late," he agreed. "Good night, Mrs. Ryan. It was nice meeting you."

"Good night. Enjoy yourselves."

That night Caitlin and Laurence did have a lot of fun. They went to a movie in Middletown, then afterward to a pizza place where they laughed and talked about Highgate.

"You know, we should have gotten to know each other better last year, Laurence," Caitlin mused. "Remember the fund-raiser? You were incredible."

He laughed and shook his head. "I did look kind of weird in my princess outfit."

"But you won! It was a great costume, and the best part was that no one knew you were entering. Why'd you do it? I've always wondered."

"I don't know. I guess I could say it was for a good cause. But the real reason was that Emily talked me into it."

"She did? She never told me!"

"I told her I'd choke her if she said a word to anyone. It would have ruined all the fun."

"Well, you helped make the whole show, Laurence."

"Thanks, Caitlin," he said good-naturedly.

Their talk of the fund-raiser and the year past reminded Caitlin of Diana and how she'd halfheartedly tried to get Diana involved on one of the committees just to get closer to Jed. How awful she'd been—only using Diana. She felt sorry about it now.

"I'm going to miss Diana," Caitlin said thoughtfully.

"You know," Laurence said seriously, "I always worried about her at Highgate. I was the one who told her to try getting in on scholarship. Her brother and I were really good friends before he died. I sort of adopted her after that. She was feeling lost, and, being an only child, I liked the idea of being big brother to her." He took a sip of soda. "But she never did fit in. She was afraid that everyone thought she didn't belong, and she was too shy to make a lot of new friends."

"I really should have tried to help her back then."

Laurence shrugged. "She's going to do okay, I think, from now on."

During the rest of the evening, they talked about all the things they had in common. To their mutual surprise they discovered that aside from their love of horses, they'd both attended the same sailing school on Chesapeake Bay and they'd both spent summers in Europe and winter-vacationed in the Caribbean.

It was fairly late when they returned to Ryan Acres, so Laurence said good night to her at the door. His hands on her shoulders, he leaned over and gave her a gentle kiss.

"It's been a good night," he said quietly. "I really had a great time, Caitlin."

"So did I." She was amazed that she meant it. For hours, she hadn't thought of Jed at all, though the pain was still there just under the surface. If she allowed herself to think about him—of how it had felt to be held in *his* arms—she knew she'd fall apart.

There probably never would be anyone who had all the things that Jed had that were so right for her—all the things that melted her heart and made her knees weak when she looked at him, heard his voice, saw his smile, watched his athletic body in action on the soccer field or on the back of a horse. With Jed there'd been something extra—something that had kept her awake at night thinking of him, something that couldn't stop her from loving him, even now when he'd made it clear that he never wanted to have anything to do with her again.

But Laurence was a wonderful person, too, and she decided then, as he stood with his arm around her shoulder, that she wasn't going to let her thoughts of Jed stand in the way of getting to know Laurence much better.

On Sunday, when Regina Ryan heard that Caitlin was spending the day with Laurence, she raised no objections.

"Have a good time, dear," was all she said as Caitlin climbed into her car, which Rollins had parked in front of the main entrance for her. Margaret had helped pack up the small storage space behind the driver's seat with the baskets of

food Caitlin would be bringing and had added a
cooler of soda on the front seat. "I'll see you this
evening. Bring Laurence back, if you wish."

Caitlin had driven off with mixed emotions. Her
grandmother obviously approved of Laurence. It
was no surprise why. He was kind, intelligent,
polite, and from a good family Regina Ryan had
known and admired for years. He was everything
her grandmother could have hoped for. But Caitlin
wondered if she ever could care for him the way
she had Jed.

Jed had everything that was right for Caitlin in a
different way. He could go out and rope cattle on
his father's ranch. He could camp under the stars
in the hills in a sleeping bag, yet look gorgeous in a
suit and dance as if the night had no end. He could
charm anyone.

But the one thing Jed couldn't do was what she
still longed for despite all that had happened—Jed
couldn't love her anymore!

Caitlin swung her car up the winding roads of
the state park, toward the place she and Laurence
had chosen for their picnic. She willed herself to
erase Jed from her thoughts. She wouldn't let him
ruin her day with Laurence.

The park was high in the mountains bordering
West Virginia, in an area of tall pines and oaks.
Caitlin found the picnic area without too much
trouble and pulled her car in. She set up the
blanket, baskets, and soda on a spot near the edge
of the outcropping overlooking the mountains
beyond. She wanted this to be a special day for

Diana. She'd brought a couple of cushions so Diana wouldn't be uncomfortable, and she took these, too, from the back of her car.

Soon she heard voices coming up the path behind her and turned quickly to face them. Smiling brightly, she called out, "Diana! Laurence." She started walking toward her two friends who were coming up the path and entering the clearing.

"Caitlin, what are you doing here?"

"Surprise!" Caitlin said. "Laurence and I thought a walk in the park might make you hungry." She pointed to the picnic spread.

"Oh, Caitlin, it looks lovely. You shouldn't have," Diana said excitedly.

"We wanted to." Laurence grinned.

"You look great," Caitlin added. "And it must feel good to get out of the hospital."

"And how." Diana was wearing the pink blouse Laurence had given her and a pair of white cotton slacks. She'd put on enough weight in the past weeks so that the clothing no longer hung loosely on her frame.

"I brought you some pillows." Caitlin led Diana to a spot near the blanket, where the sunlight came through the pines. Although it had been hot down in the valley, the mountain air was much cooler.

"This makes me feel like a real human being again!" Diana exclaimed.

"What have your doctors told you?" Caitlin asked. "You said yesterday you'd be talking to them."

"They think I can go home the middle of next week. That'll give me time to get ready for school."

"The summer's going so fast," Caitlin said. "I can't believe it."

"You've been busy," Laurence reminded her. "You girls want a soda?"

"Sure," Caitlin said. She sat down on the blanket near Diana.

Diana nodded, too. "I wish you hadn't had to leave the hospital," she said sadly to Caitlin. "I've missed your visits."

"I have, too, but my grandmother insisted. She never knew I was volunteering—I guess I told you that."

"But it was for a good cause." Laurence joined them, handed the girls their sodas, and sat down next to Caitlin. "She probably understands that."

Caitlin hadn't told them that she'd never told her grandmother about Diana being at the hospital or her own responsibility for Ian Foster's accident. She still didn't have the courage to do so.

"So I'll bet you're anxious to get to that new school," she said to Diana.

Diana grinned. "They're offering all the courses I want, and even my mother isn't making a fuss about my going to another private school. She never thought Highgate was a good idea, you know."

"That's okay. It'll be different this time," Caitlin said.

"You two will try to come visit me on one of the long weekends, won't you?" Diana asked. "It's not all that far to Pennsylvania."

"Sure will!" Caitlin agreed.

"I don't know about you two," Laurence interrupted, "but I'm starved! What's in this basket, Caitlin?"

"Let's see, that should be the fried chicken, and Margaret made up a batch of biscuits. They should still be warm. The pies are in the other basket, and the cole slaw and fruit are in the bag. I'll get the paper plates and napkins."

Within a few minutes they all had filled their plates.

"Being out in the fresh air really did make me hungry." Diana laughed as she bit into her chicken.

"Good!" Laurence and Caitlin said with one breath. "Keep eating."

"I feel like a little kid with two baby-sitters," Diana joked.

They laughed and talked casually until nearly all the food was gone and all of them felt stuffed.

"While you girls talk," Laurence spoke up as he deposited his empty plate in the plastic bag Caitlin had brought along, "I'm going to go look for some kindling for a fire."

"What for? It's not that cold out."

"But what would a picnic be without toasted marshmallows? I brought a bag along, and there's a little fireplace right over there. I'll be right back."

Caitlin finished clearing up, then glanced down at Diana, who was sitting cross-legged on her cushions. "I got a letter from Ian's mother yesterday. He'll be coming home from that school they sent him to."

"So he's getting better, too?" Diana asked hopefully.

Caitlin sighed and shook her head. "There really hasn't been much improvement, but he's been homesick and they think he might do better with his family around," she said. "I thought you'd want to know."

"Thanks," Diana said. "And, Caitlin, don't lose hope."

A momentary flicker of pain crossed Caitlin's face. Then looking around she asked, "Say, what about a walk? Think you're up to it?"

"Why not?" Diana quickly got to her feet. "I might as well start getting some exercise."

"Good. There's a path over there."

"I wanted to talk to you, anyway," Diana said as they started away under the pines. "I didn't want Laurence to overhear." She paused thoughtfully. "What do you think of him?"

"I like him a lot. He's a really nice person."

"I was glad to hear you two went out."

Caitlin smiled. "I had a great time."

"Laurence really likes you, too," Diana added. "He says he wishes he'd gotten to know you better a long time ago. You seem to get along well together."

"We do. And my grandmother's already asked him to come riding with us."

"She likes him, too, then?"

"Yes. She's known his family for a long time."

"Great," Diana said. "It's none of my business, but I hope you keep seeing him back at Highgate."

Caitlin hadn't honestly thought that far ahead. She didn't want to think about returning there just yet—it meant returning to Jed.

"You're not looking forward to going back, are you?" Diana asked, glancing over at Caitlin's worried face.

"Not really. It'll be different this year."

"Jed?"

"Yes. It'll be uncomfortable being around him."

"There was something else I wanted to tell you. It—it has to do with him."

Caitlin was instantly alert. She knew that deep inside she still hadn't given up hope. *But how foolish*, she thought. *Jed isn't going to change his mind.*

Diana's next words pretty much confirmed that. "I called him after you and I talked. I know you told me not to, but I thought he should know."

"And what did he say?"

"He said he was glad you'd told me but that it didn't change his mind. I told him he was being thickheaded and stupid—that everybody makes mistakes." Diana took a breath.

"I think he still cares about you, Caitlin, but I think you're right in forgetting about him and starting over. It may take him a long time to come around."

"I know," Caitlin whispered, trying to hide the pain and anger she felt inside. Even after all she'd tried to do to make amends he couldn't forgive her. Who gave him the right to be so self-righteous? she wondered. "I'm trying to forget—and I have Laurence to thank for that. He's been so nice to me."

"Stick with him. He's a wonderful person. He knows about Jed, too, and says he'll be patient."

"He did?"

"Don't tell him I told you!"

"I won't." Caitlin looked over to the sandy-haired girl. "You're such a good friend, Diana. I wish we'd gotten to know each other sooner, too."

Diana only smiled and linked her arm with Caitlin's. "Maybe we should head back. Laurence probably has the wood by now."

They returned to the picnic site, where Laurence had started a fire and was in the process of gathering sticks for the marshmallows. "Here, take these," he said, handing foot-long hickory twigs to the two girls.

As the three of them sat around the fire, Caitlin looked at Laurence. *I could learn to love him*, she thought. The idea did not displease her. Feeling her gaze, Laurence looked up at her and, smiling, took her hand and clasped it gently in his.

19

"You'll stay in touch?" Caitlin asked as she hugged Diana.

Diana had been discharged from the hospital two days before, and Caitlin and Laurence had taken her to a celebration dinner at a local steak house. They'd had a great night, but both girls were teary eyed as they stood in the parking lot to say good-bye.

"I'll write once a week," Diana said firmly.

"Me, too," Caitlin said. "And no more diets! Promise?"

Diana laughed, then blinked away her tears. "Thanks, Caitlin, for everything. I'm so glad we got to be friends."

"I'm glad, too—and don't thank me." Caitlin sighed as she felt the old twinges of guilt return. How could Diana be so forgiving. Deep inside, Caitlin knew her debt to Diana still wasn't paid—and perhaps never would be. She shook her head to push away the thoughts. "I'm going to miss you."

"We'll get together as soon as we can."

"Yes."

Diana hesitated, then whispered in Caitlin's ea "I hope it works out for you and Laurence."

"He's good for me." *Maybe better than I deserve* Caitlin added to herself silently.

"I'd better go. Laurence is waiting, and m parents will be worried if I stay out too late."

After Caitlin said her good-byes and made plan to see Laurence the next day, she stood by her ca and watched them drive away. She felt so sa seeing Diana go. Helping her had been the on thing that had kept Caitlin from collapsing afte losing Jed. Now, she dreaded going back to High gate and seeing him again. It would be like havin a knife stuck in her heart every time he ignore her.

Suddenly Laurence seemed like the only perso she could cling to. Laurence knew what she' done, had forgiven her, and would stand besid her. She needed that sense of security right now She'd been deserted twice; first by her father, the by Jed. She couldn't bear to be left alone again

Of course, Ginny would be at Highgate, and i would be so good to see her again. But, sh reminded herself, Ginny didn't know the truth about the terrible secret she'd kept. Despite he urge to push the feeling away, the old surge of guil surfaced again. Would it always be there, smother ing her, keeping her apart from the people sh cared about?

She didn't want to have to hide things any

more—she didn't want any more horrible secrets in her life! She just wanted to be like everyone else.

Finally she opened the door of her sports car and climbed behind the wheel.

For the rest of summer vacation Caitlin and Laurence saw each other often. He was always sweet and thoughtful and didn't let a day go by without calling her. His genuine concern for her showed in the warmth of his voice. Probably most importantly, he was always considerate of her feelings and needs.

"Did you have a good day?" he asked during one of his calls.

"Mmm. I worked in the stables most of the afternoon."

"Getting Duster ready for his trip back to Highgate?"

"And helping Jeff. I haven't been around the horses too much this summer. It feels good to get out there."

"You deserve it. You've worked hard enough the last couple of months."

Caitlin could almost see his smile over the phone line.

"I'll pick you up for tennis in the morning," he said.

"Great."

"Have a good night, and say hello to your grandmother for me."

"I will. She was just asking about you."

"You told her good things, I hope." He laughed
"What else could I tell her?"

Caitlin was grateful to Laurence for anothe
reason. Mrs. Ryan thought the world of him, an
Caitlin never had felt she'd had her grandmother
approval so completely. It made a big difference i
their relationship. Much of the stress and strai
between grandmother and granddaughter wa
gone now, and Caitlin felt as though a burden ha
been taken off her shoulders. As she spent com
fortable hours over dinner talking to her granc
mother, making plans for Laurence and his famil
to join them at Ryan Acres for an afternoon rid
she finally got the attention she'd been craving a
her life. At last, she felt that she had a real home
Her feelings for her grandmother were softening
and she wanted to do nothing to change their nev
rapport.

Mrs. Ryan had a present for her the followin
day. She came home from the mine with a large
wrapped box and insisted Caitlin open it immed
ately.

Caitlin tore away the wrapping paper and lifte
the cover. A chic, white satin gown was inside

"Oh, it's beautiful! It's the dress I saw th
Saturday we were in Georgetown," Caitlin criec
"But you said it was too old for me!"

"I've changed my mind." The older woma
smiled. "You've grown up this summer, my dear.
thought you might like to wear it tomorrow eve
ning. I've invited Laurence and his parents to hav
dinner with us at the club." Regina Ryan stoo

back to admire her granddaughter as Caitlin held
the dress up in front of her. "I thought to set it off,
you might like to wear my black pearls."

"Oh, Grandmother, do you mean it? They would
be perfect—absolutely perfect!"

"I'd like to see you wear them. They've been in
the Ryan family for generations. It's time they were
passed on to you."

As Caitlin dressed for dinner the next evening,
she fastened the long strands of pearls around her
neck. She felt gorgeous. The sleek, smooth lines of
the long dress were perfect on her tall, well-
proportioned frame, and the pearls added an extra
touch of glamour.

Her grandmother smiled approvingly as Caitlin
came down the stairs into the front hall where
Laurence and his parents were waiting. The look in
Laurence's eyes when he saw her left Caitlin
feeling warm all over.

"You're beautiful," he whispered as he handed
her a long white box.

Caitlin quickly opened the box. "How did you
know how much I loved roses?" she cried, lifting
the blossoms to her nose.

"Pretty flowers for a pretty woman." He
grinned.

Two days before they were due to go back to
Highgate, she and Laurence spent the day at Ryan
Acres. The afternoon was hot, and they'd decided
to take a walk in the woods rather than go out
riding in the heat.

"Did you get everything packed?" Laurence asked her.

"Almost. I'm going shopping in Georgetown with my grandmother tomorrow, and that'll be it. What about you?"

"Pretty much. The books will be the worst. I'll get my car packed tomorrow, then I can come help you with yours."

"But you've got so much to do yourself!"

He smiled. "I don't mind." His voice was soft and he reached over to take her hand. When he squeezed it gently, she returned the pressure.

They walked a few minutes in silence. Laurence seemed thoughtful.

"Is something wrong?" Caitlin finally asked.

"No, not wrong. I wanted to talk to you and was trying to think of the right words."

Caitlin's stomach lurched. So many bad things had happened to her lately, she could only think the worse. Was he going to tell her he didn't want to see her anymore?

But when they reached a clearing in the woods where a stream trickled despite the dry summer, he stopped and turned toward her, taking her other hand. The look in his eyes was as warm and caring as ever.

"I wanted to ask you something," he said softly, his cheeks a little flushed from nervousness. "I know we haven't been going out together all that long, but I really care about you."

"I care about you, too."

"I've never asked a girl to—to go with me before."

196

I'm . . . I'm not really sure how to do it. But all I know is that you're the only girl I want to be with."

Caitlin's heart leaped. She looked up at Laurence's face. He was waiting expectantly, nervously, for her response.

Slowly Caitlin smiled. "And I want to be with you, too, Laurence," she whispered at last.

"You do?" He seemed hardly able to believe he'd heard her correctly. Then he grinned. "Oh, Caitlin." He hugged her close, pressing his cheek against the top of her head. In a moment he tilted up her chin and kissed her softly.

"It's going to be a good year," he said huskily.

"Yes," she murmured. But even as she snuggled her head against his shoulder, she thought of Jed. As hard as she tried to forget him, he was always there in the back of her mind. She knew she loved him as much as ever, but in that moment she promised herself she'd never let Laurence know. He deserved better than that, and she'd *never* admit to him how she feared her first meeting with Jed in the fall, knowing it was going to tear her heart out to see him.

She pressed her cheek more closely against Laurence's shirt and let him hold her until the tears the thought of Jed had brought disappeared from her eyes.

"We'll make it a good year," she said at last. *And I won't hurt you, Laurence*, she thought. *No matter what happens, I'm finished with causing people pain.*

Perhaps with Laurence her monstrous guilt would finally go away. She sighed and let him kiss her again. Yes, Laurence was peace and a safe haven.

But, oh, how she dreaded that first day back at Highgate!

FRANCINE PASCAL

In addition to collaborating on the Broadway musical *George M!* and the nonfiction book *The Strange Case of Patty Hearst*, Francine Pascal has written an adult novel, *Save Johanna!*, and four young adult novels, *Hangin' Out with Cici, My First Love and Other Disasters, The Hand-Me-Down Kid*, and *Love and Betrayal & Hold the Mayo!* She is also the creator of the Sweet Valley High series. Ms. Pascal has three daughters, Jamie, Susan, and Laurie, and lives in New York City.

JOANNA CAMPBELL

As a teenager in Connecticut, Joanna Campbell was an enthusiastic reader who especially loved books about horses. An accomplished horsewoman herself, Ms. Campbell also sings and plays the piano professionally. She and her two teenaged children live in a seacoast town in Maine, where Joanna owns an antique store and writes young adult novels (many of which feature her old love, horses!).

Caitlin

LOVING introduced Caitlin—the irresistibly charming, dazzlingly rich, Alexis Colby of the teen set. Whatever Caitlin wants—she goes for—and usually gets. In LOVING, Caitlin wants handsome Jed Michaels. And the sparks really fly when Jed falls in love with someone else.

Now comes **LOVE LOST**. School's out and it looks like the summer will be a paradise for young lovers. But when tragedy strikes and Caitlin's world turns upside down, will she come forward and risk losing the most important thing in her life?

And coming soon—**TRUE LOVE**. Things just aren't working out the way Caitlin wants them to, no matter what she tries! Will it take a disaster to get certain people to see her point? Read the third exciting installment of the Caitlin trilogy—coming in December, 1985—and find out for yourself!

C13-9/85

☐	25143	**POWER PLAY #4**	$2.50
☐	25043	**ALL NIGHT LONG #5**	$2.50
☐	25105	**DANGEROUS LOVE #6**	$2.50
☐	25106	**DEAR SISTER #7**	$2.50
☐	25092	**HEARTBREAKER #8**	$2.50
☐	25026	**RACING HEARTS #9**	$2.50
☐	25016	**WRONG KIND OF GIRL #10**	$2.50
☐	25046	**TOO GOOD TO BE TRUE #11**	$2.50
☐	25035	**WHEN LOVE DIES #12**	$2.50
☐	24524	**KIDNAPPED #13**	$2.25
☐	24531	**DECEPTIONS #14**	$2.50
☐	24582	**PROMISES #15**	$2.50
☐	24672	**RAGS TO RICHES #16**	$2.50
☐	24723	**LOVE LETTERS #17**	$2.50
☐	24825	**HEAD OVER HEELS #18**	$2.50
☐	24893	**SHOWDOWN #19**	$2.50
☐	24947	**CRASH LANDING! #20**	$2.50
☐	24994	**RUNAWAY #21**	$2.50
☐	25133	**TOO MUCH IN LOVE #22**	$2.50

Prices and availability subject to change without notice.

Buy them at your local bookstore or use this handy coupon for ordering:

Bantam Books, Inc., Dept SVH, 414 East Golf Road, Des Plaines, Ill. C0016

Please send me the books I have checked above. I am enclosing $_____
(please add $1.25 to cover postage and handling). Send check or money order
—no cash or C.O.D.'s please.

Mr/Mrs/Miss _____

Address_____

City_____ State/Zip_____

SVH—9/85

Please allow four to six weeks for delivery. This offer expires 3/86.

SPECIAL
MONEY SAVING
OFFER

Now you can have an up-to-date listing of Bantam's hundreds of titles plus take advantage of our unique and exciting bonus book offer. A special offer which gives you the opportunity to purchase a Bantam book for only 50¢. Here's how!

By ordering any five books at the regular price per order, you can also choose any other single book listed (up to a $4.95 value) for just 50¢. Some restrictions do apply, but for further details why not send for Bantam's listing of titles today!

Just send us your name and address plus 50¢ to defray the postage and handling costs.